TRAVELS WITH NANDIGHOSH

Demystifying Krishna

Satish Mutatkar & Yeshwant Marathe

Popular Prakashan
www.popularprakashan.com

Published by
Harsha Bhatkal for
POPULAR PRAKASHAN PVT. LTD.
301, Mahalaxmi Chambers
22, Bhulabhai Desai Road
Mumbai - 400 026
info@popularprakashan.com

First Published 2023

(4547)
ISBN: 978-81-958324-7-7

Cover design: Milind Ghaisas
Layout: Anjali Sawant
Typesetting: Satyawan Rane

Printed In India
by Brigar Media Pvt. Ltd.
Ahmedabad 380004

Contents

Foreword

I have read the book *Travels with Nandighosh: Demystifying Krishna* with interest. It is a delightful account of a couple of friends travelling in a camper on a journey through South India taking in ancient archaeological sites and the countryside that varies from rice fields carpeted in green as far as the eye can see to ancient temples in the southern part of the great Indian plateau.

It is a unique travelogue which discusses fascinating incidents in the life of Lord Krishna — a fresh and unique look at the mythology, history and heritage of India. A charming trip of discovery in short.

As travelogues go it is a wonderfully readable book that makes you want to get into your travel gear and do this enriching trip on your next vacation; a must for your bucket list.

Shyam Benegal

Preface

Some seeds germinate quickly while others take longer and this could be said about books too. The seeds of this book can perhaps be traced back over a decade and more, even before the authors decided to join forces.

Like most Indians, we too have been fascinated by the great Indian epic Mahabharat. Once upon a time there used to be passionate discussions among aficionados about whether it should be called Mythology or History. With the availability of computer generated data going back tens of thousands of years, much of that debate seems to be settled since there is a high degree of correlation between the astronomical observations mentioned in ancient texts and what the computers tell us. Clearly there is a core of History in the epic, with perhaps many layers of padding added in subsequent renditions. May be it is time to introduce a new term, *histomythology*, to describe the mix. At any rate, it gives rise to many questions, none more intriguing than about the events in the life of everyone's favourite, Krishna.

Krishna has been written about for a few thousand years and many versions of his life can be seen in literature and folklore. Therein lies a challenge. There was a time when the written word was sacrosanct but if there is one thing that the age of social media has taught us, it is to be a little sceptical about all reports. Even if they are about an event which might have happened yesterday, leave aside something which may have occurred thousands of years ago.

Amazingly our ancestors were alive to the problem and welcomed questioning minds and attitudes. Prashna Upnishad 4.9 says:

ऐष हि द्रष्ट स्प्रष्टा श्रोता घ्राता रसयिता मन्ता बोद्धा कर्ता विज्ञानात्मा पुरुषः।
स परेऽक्षर आत्मनि संप्रतिष्टते

Meaning, *it is he who beholds, touches, hears, smells, tastes, perceives, thinks, reasons, conceives, acts, whose essence is knowledge, the Self. He becomes merged in the Supreme, undecaying Âtman.*

Clearly, the message was that anyone who seeks *knowledge* is encouraged to use all his senses and the power of reasoning to understand things better.

The beauty about the culture, the civilisation, the heritage that our ancestors have gifted to us is that it allows us to freely visualise possible alternate scenarios and explanations for events which may have happened in the distant past. It is in this spirit that this book is being presented to readers.

A book of fiction needs no bibliography and we aren't appending any, although very conscious efforts were made to rely on more trustworthy source material. The 19 volumes on Mahabharata so painstakingly produced by Bhandarkar Oriental Research Institute (BORI), the 12 volumes of the first English translation of Mahabharat by K.M. Ganguli published from 1893 to 1896, as also copious writings by many scholars in English and Marathi jostling for space on our bookshelves bear testimony to the authors' passion.

And finally, a caveat: there is absolutely no need for readers to agree with anything in the text, either by way of an assumption or analysis or inference. If the book merely serves to provoke the reader into asking a few questions of his own and embarking on a search for some answers, our efforts would have been amply rewarded.

Bon voyage, happy journey, शुभास्ते सन्तु पन्थानः।

Acknowledgements

We are immensely grateful to:

Mr. Shyam Benegal, doyen of India's Film and TV Industries, Padma Bhushan and Dadasaheb Phalke Awards recipient and winner of countless film awards, for having appreciated the book and consented to write the foreword.

Stalwarts from the fields of Entertainment, Education, Medicine and Commerce for providing valuable feedback and priceless words landing the effort (in alphabetical order): Ananth Mahadevan, Dr. Aniruddha Pandit, Dr. Avinash Phadke, Bharat Dabholkar and Rakesh Verma.

Milind Ghaisas of Adived Advertising for the cover design,

Aneesh Date for the sketches.

Mallika Noorani and Shruti Tandon of Parinam Law Associates for legal advice,

and

M/S Popular Prakashan for publishing the book with all the editing, proof reading and marketing help that it entails.

Thank you all ever so much, we will remain indebted forever.

Nandighosh
DATE.

Prologue

He walked towards the gleaming two-door vanity van standing in his bungalow compound with the same tingling sensation he used to have as a child, 60 years ago, while looking at a new toy car. But this was no toy, it was the real deal and more. He started to examine its luxurious interiors with growing satisfaction. Strange, he thought, a few months ago I wasn't even aware of vanity vans or camper trailers in India.

***

A few months ago Dhananjay Kuru had been despondent. He had been eagerly looking forward to retirement at 65 and travelling throughout the country. He had sold off his transport business with its fleet of 80 school buses, just as he had told his family he would a few years earlier. His wife Neeta, daughter Meera and son-in-law Naresh had not really believed him when he had first mentioned it. But when DK, as he was universally known, announced it as a done deal at his lavish 65th birthday party, all assembled friends and relatives had applauded enthusiastically. Now Neeta and I are free to explore every inch of the country and absorb the marvellous stories carved in stone in every corner just as per our dream, he had announced, as Neeta looked on proudly and happily.

But sometimes man proposes and nature disposes. Within a fortnight of returning to USA, Meera had called informing them of her pregnancy. Pregnant after eight years of marriage. Before they could really begin to celebrate the prospect of welcoming their long awaited first grandchild, Meera cautioned them: there were a few complications, nothing really to worry about but doctors had advised complete bed rest. Neeta left for USA a few days later. I might as well do a few solo trips locally, DK had thought to himself and started checking out dates and destinations with travel sites. Then Covid-19 struck and strict lockdowns were enforced everywhere.

Isolated in his huge bungalow in Juhu, DK turned to his library and dusted off a few books he had always meant to read. Instead of comforting him in his solitude tomes on Ramayan and Mahabharat made him more restless. Not a particularly religious man, DK had been visiting the local Ram temple and the ISKCON temple every week for years, more to keep Neeta happy than out of any real conviction. Why were Ram and Krishna, both *avataars* of Vishnu, so different, he wondered. One trying to be the Ideal Man, the other ready to cut some corners for a perceived larger good. He smiled wryly as he thought of a conundrum from the book *Catch-22*, which had stayed with him since his college days: If God was all powerful and all good, why did he invent toothache? Either he was not 'good' enough to have avoided creating it or he was not 'powerful' enough to have prevented its creation. Anyway, some God had surely been good enough to look after him, he thought, allowing him a happy exit from his business a little before the pandemic struck, bringing all valuations in transport industry crashing down.

Months went by. The country was thrown into chaos with flights and trains grounded. DK, not used to being at home or being alone or being without work, became more and more irritable. He took his morning walks in his compound but he was really not too fond of gardening; the greenery and the flowers did little to mitigate his restlessness. The couple who did the housekeeping and cooking, and who had been provided residential quarters over the garage, started looking at him with concern, so he consciously tried to clamp down on his snapping. Neeta was getting daily reports, he was sure. The bland *Upma* and white of boiled eggs he got for breakfast on most days, instead of his favourite *Aloo Parathas*, were a dead giveaway as to who was deciding the menu.

He turned to the large smart TV they had installed just the previous year for solace. News channels were depressing but OTT platforms were a saving grace. It was while flipping through OTT platforms for old movies that he had, what he would later call, his 'Light Bulb' moment. Shah Rukh Khan's *Swades*, one of his favourites, was playing but more than the hero, he froze at the sight of that vehicle.

If Shah Rukh can drive one, why can't I, he thought! I even have a Heavy Vehicle driving license, the original 40 year old one — he smiled at the memory of the first school bus he had bought — having been renewed periodically by his staff. This might be the answer I have been looking for he thought excitedly as the idea grew. Road travel seemed to be the only practical way of getting out of his confinement and travelling in a camper or a van also bypassed hotels which might or might not be sanitised properly, if they were operational at all in the first place.

A couple of telephone calls to friends in the film industry got him leads of companies supplying vanity vans. 'No problem sir, we can have it configured any way you want — one door, two doors, three doors.' A door referred to a tiny, compact bedroom, DK learnt. 'Latest Japanese fixtures with every bathroom Sir. We have a new chassis, new engine available, and we can deliver your van with all the papers within four weeks. Fuel tank loaded to the full, if you wish.' Lucky me, he thought, I don't have to worry about the right side of a menu card or any Rate Card anymore and started to work on his wish list for his dream camper.

Should I get a driver or drive myself? Drive myself, he thought, Shah Rukh's image was too powerful. But then driving alone might get boring, why not ask some friend to join or get a companion to share the load? The loneliness was beginning to get to him, he admitted to himself, and an intelligent companion would be a big relief.

It would have to be a two door camper, with ample storage space for clothes and linen. He drew the sketch on a piece of paper, tore it, drew again and at the end of it was tickled by his own design. Next morning he placed the order. 'You want a name for it, Sir? We can have it made in stainless steel in impressive italicised letters.' 'Call it nandighosh,' he had said. DK could not remember where he had read the name but it sounded impressive.

Now to look for a companion, he thought, and sent out messages in his friends' WhatsApp groups. No volunteers raised their hands, but there were plenty of thumbs-up and applause emojis for his idea. Many suggestions too, 'go on a safari'; 'go to Kedarnath'; 'go to Puri'. He had no intention of going onto any small roads, certainly not to begin with, and wanted to stick to the main highways. At least they are open, fuel and food won't be a problem.

One suggestion touched a chord with him instantly — Srirangam in Tamil Nadu. As the location of the largest functioning Vishnu temple in India, he might find the answers to his queries there; after all both Ram and Krishna were *avataars* of Vishnu.

The lack of progress on the companion hunt started bothering him in a couple of weeks and then he thought of Ahuja. He was the owner of Mumbai's largest driver-aggregator platform, and over the years they had developed a useful rapport since DK's company had often needed substitute or shift drivers.

"*Fikar not DKji*," Ahuja's voice had boomed over the phone. "We have the largest database of drivers in Mumbai, over 4000 of them, and we have affiliates all over India. You want a driver who speaks four languages in Gangtok, we will find him for you", he had promised.

"No, someone who speaks Hindi and English will do; but I am looking for a travelling companion while driving to Tamil Nadu, not just a driver with a Heavy Vehicle driving license. Someone I should be able to converse with, on an equal basis. And I need him by Monday morning."

"Not to worry *DKji, mil jaayega.* At least a post-graduate from a good family, I promise you. We have many in our database and many more have joined since the lockdown. I will call you."

Ahuja had been true to his word. He had called two days earlier on Friday. "*Mil gaya DKji, aapka companion.* He returned to India after working for a few years in USA and joined an Ayurveda factory up north. He took voluntary retirement sometime back from a very senior position to pursue his interest in Ancient India. He has travelled all over the country and recently submitted his PhD thesis on 'Customs and Practices of Ancient India'. He was planning to go to Tamil Nadu, but got stuck in Mumbai due to Covid and then he saw our Ad on social media."

"Sounds excellent Ahuja. But what about a Heavy Vehicle driving license and a RT-PCR test?"

"*Sirji, ye Ahuja ka kaam hai!* This gentleman Thakur, that's his name, had worked with UPS in USA driving delivery trucks to earn some money as a student. His Indian license is valid till 2024. And his RT-PCR test has been done, report should come tomorrow."

"Sounds fantastic Ahuja, I knew I could rely on you. Ask him to meet me Monday at 8.30 am. And thanks a ton!"

***

Clothes check, toiletries check; medicines, sanitiser bottles, masks check. Loaded FastTag check. Satisfied, DK gave one last loving look to the beautiful camper, and strode back to his bungalow, excitement mounting at the thought of the adventure about to begin. There was a bit of tension and fear too. It had taken a lot of persuasion for Neeta to green light the trip, but she also knew that DK would be fretting under virtual house arrest. He had promised to avoid crowds, not to miss his morning walks and also to call every evening. In any case, the trip would enable him to pray at the largest Vishnu temple in the world for Meera and the baby — that had been his clinching argument and it had won the day.

❑❑❑

CHAPTER 1

Baby Steps

"The toughest part of going anywhere from Mumbai by road is getting out of Mumbai itself," said DK as he tried to change lanes. Traffic had become unruly since he had last driven on Mumbai roads and half the city seemed to have been dug up for the much awaited Metro. A few of the earlier strict Covid restrictions had been relaxed, but local trains were still not allowed to operate. It seemed to DK that a majority of Mumbai was back on the streets. He stole a quick glance at his fellow passenger and admitted to himself that he was a very impressive person indeed. He smiled as he recalled his fears of last night.

DK had woken up at 4.30 in the morning with a slight headache. He had checked his BP with the BP machine, 140/90. Slightly high but not enough to call up Doctor Shah. He had checked his blood sugar. At 115, it was also slightly high but nothing alarming. He had sighed and asked himself the question he had been deliberately avoiding asking himself. Was he just tense and nervous about his companion for the trip? Had he been needlessly impulsive and rash in planning the trip under the present tough conditions with an unknown companion? Was he letting himself in for a few days of torture? He had gone out on the lawn, walked around for a while and as darkness gave way to light, his anxiety started melting away.

I am glad I trusted Ahuja, DK thought as *nandighosh* crossed the first toll post at Vashi. He glanced at the calm figure in the passenger seat as they headed towards the Mumbai-Pune expressway and looked at his wrist watch. It was just over an hour earlier that DK had opened the door in response to the gentle chiming of the doorbell. Tall, dark, very muscular looking, very well dressed, the most striking feature in the handsome face of the stranger were his eyes. The attractive twinkle instantly broke barriers.

"My name is Jagganath Thakur," the newcomer introduced himself with a smile.

"Yes, I have been waiting for you. Let us get going first, we can talk on the way. You can call me DK, like everyone in my world does."

"Works for me. And you are welcome to call me JT."

DK had just added a small bag with his BP machine and the blood sugar monitoring kit to his luggage which he had already checked last evening. The newcomer's small bag was kept in the 'bedroom' meant for him and he moved into the front passenger seat as DK took the driver's seat. He wanted to try out *nandighosh* first. As DK eased it into first gear, he got the comfortable feel an ace jockey gets with a well-trained, powerful mount under him.

"So JT," said DK, the name rolling off his tongue easily, "let us set the ground rules for the trip first. We are in no hurry to reach anywhere. I am a retired man with plenty of time on my hand and getting out of Mumbai during Covid times is a huge relief. So, this is going to be a leisurely trip. Seven days or ten days it makes little difference to me, in fact in many ways the longer the better."

"Excellent. Works for me too."

"I think we should avoid night driving as a rule. The lighting on some stretches may be poor and I am driving a heavy vehicle after many years. We will stop over at some convenient spot each evening. The next morning we will get the fuel and water tanks filled up and the van cleaned while we have our breakfast; we should be ready to hit the road by 9 o'clock. Our first stop this evening could be near Satara with a lunch break somewhere near Pune."

"Sounds like a plan DK. But where are we going?"

"Srirangam in Tamil Nadu. That is where the Sri Ranganath Swamy Temple is located. I believe it is the largest functioning Vishnu temple in the world. It should be worth a visit."

"I am sure it is," replied JT.

DK slowed down near the Khalapur toll post, but FastTags had considerably reduced the regular congestion at toll posts.

"We should be crossing Lonavala soon."

"Pretty place!"

"There is an Ekvira Aai Temple somewhere around here. I always meant to see it with my wife, Neeta. But I was too busy with work till recently."

"It is an interesting temple. Legend has it that during the Pandavas' *vanvaas*, Ekvira Devi appeared before them and commanded them to build the temple. She also ordered them to do it overnight. So they worked feverishly throughout the night but accomplished the task in time."

"How did they manage that?" DK wondered.

"If China can build hospitals quickly, why couldn't Indians have built a modest sized temple overnight? There is so much we do not know yet about the technology in existence then."

"Fascinating!" DK exclaimed. "I love ancient architecture, though I have not seen as much in India as I would have liked. Always meant to see these places with Neeta after retirement but then fate intervened. We are expecting our first grandchild soon, so Neeta had to go to USA," DK said very proudly.

"Congratulations to all of you DK. A new addition to the family energises everyone."

"What about your family JT?"

"*Vasudhaiv Kutumbakam!* All the world is my family, but if you are asking about immediate blood relatives, I am afraid no one is left."

"Oh sorry to hear that. But you are also interested in epics, mythology and stories from our scriptures, I understand?" DK quickly changed the subject.

JT smiled. "Yes of course. Who isn't? Plus, of course, I have been to a few places and have been with a few people up north who have practically spent their days and nights immersed in the epics."

"*Tab toh khoob jamegi*!" DK was very thrilled now with Ahuja's choice. "I love our epics, Ramayan and Mahabharat, and got interested in the characters of Ram and Krishna, but there are a few contradictions in their personalities and stories which have been bothering me."

"Maybe we can talk about them as we go along. Discussions always help and we will also be able to pass the time comfortably."

DK continued with his theme. "How are the two so different, although both are *avataars* of Vishnu? In fact, that is why I thought of visiting Srirangam, the largest functioning temple of Vishnu Bhagwan in India, and see if the head priest or someone else there can provide some satisfactory answers."

"We revere Ram and Krishna as they are believed to be endowed with divine virtues and thus capable of bringing about huge transformation. Ram is called *Maryada Purushottam* or a person who follows righteousness strictly, while Krishna is seen as *Purnavataar*, the one who possesses all 16 *kalas* or perfect qualities."

"Wonderful, sounds profound. But is Krishna really incarnate or just a super human being?"

JT laughed. "In my view, it depends on who is asking. For an average person, looking for instant solutions or answers, Krishna as an incarnation might be the perfect answer."

"But that is not satisfactory, especially if the one asking questions is a little more curious or inquisitive than the average person."

"In that case he may need to examine Krishna's life in detail, step by step, to see if tricky questions might have logical answers without needing to bring Krishna's divinity, real or imagined, into the equation."

DK agreed wholeheartedly. "Exactly what I meant. Obviously, once you label someone or something as divine, your quest stops there; you have no further reason to search. But there are so many aspects of Krishna's life which seem so patently fanciful that there may not be any choice but to bring divinity into it."

JT was sanguine. "Let us try. Let us go step by step and we can think of calling Krishna incarnate if we run into something totally inexplicable."

"That sounds reasonable. Let us go in a chronological order then. Let us start with Krishna's birth. It all sounds completely muddled up! Some *Akashvani* or prophesy that Devaki's eighth child will kill his wicked *mama*, the tyrant King Kansa; new-borns being killed; escape of Vasudev from a dungeon under a tight watch on a rainy night; the river parting magically to allow the father with his new born to cross! And how exactly did he know where to go, where he would find a new born girl and parents willing to exchange? All of it is tough to swallow for anyone with common sense; hence taking recourse to divinity as an explanation looks logical though not very satisfactory."

JT laughed. "You are right. In their anxiety to bestow divinity onto Krishna, writers have added so much *masala* to perfectly explainable events that intelligent people are bound to question them."

"What do you mean?" DK wanted to know.

"Simply that there are perfectly reasonable explanations for all these. It is there in books too, but you need to read the right ones or apply the right filters to eliminate the more outlandish explanations, use some plain logic and try and build alternate feasible, reasonable, believable scenarios."

"Alright...so tell me. Let us start with Kansa and who Devaki and Vasudev were."

"Kansa was a Yadav King of Mathura about 5000 odd years ago. Devaki was Kansa's sister, married to Vasudev. Vasudev was the leader of Vrishnis, a much less powerful subset of the otherwise powerful Yadavs."

"So far it's clear. But how much should we believe, what really might have happened?" DK posed the most fundamental of questions.

"See, estimates of the time period vary considerably; let us leave that to archaeologists and other experts for the present. They have already gathered enough evidence, including cross checking of astronomical references with computer programmes which can replicate positions of stars for thousands of years, to confirm that Mahabharat indeed has a genuine core of history. Of course a lot of extra padding has been added over time, over many iterations," explained JT.

"I am with you so far."

"Kansa was a tyrant, and many people, including some from his court, were fed up with his ways. But they were afraid of his power. And then came the prophesy about Devaki's child killing him. It is perfectly reasonable to assume that some astrologer made it, though different narrations have ascribed it sometimes to Narada Muni, sometimes to *Akashvani*, possibly with the intention of adding a divine element to Krishna's birth. You may just as well think of it as any astrologer's prophesy. Astrologers making doomsday predictions is not unknown today, it was probably not unknown back then either."

"Go on," said DK.

"So there we have Kansa, a tyrant petrified at the thought of death as per some dire prediction. To try and understand Kansa's reaction we may need to think of other tyrants we may be more familiar with."

"Like say Kim Jong-un of North Korea?"

"Or Adolf Hitler or may be even Vladimir Putin. One thing all of them have in common is their almost primal need for controlling the narrative their people get to hear."

"Yes! I have read that Putin would like his people to believe that he can wrestle and overcome bears. North Korean Kim even wants his people to believe that he is divine to the extent, that he is exempt from bodily functions like defecation or urination!"

JT smiled. "Exactly. And we need to bear that in mind as we see what Kansa's response to the danger was. His first thought was to keep Devaki and Vasudev separate, but there were practical difficulties. He was fond of his sister, he had just officiated at her wedding with much pomp and for him to keep the couple separate would surely invite public comment because it would be difficult to keep it a secret for long."

"Yes, especially if it happens immediately after a marriage." DK agreed.

"His second thought was to kill his sister but that did not seem any better. Apart from his fondness for her, if the story got out that he had killed a woman, his sister, out of fear, his hold over his people would go away in no time. Moreover, if his subjects came to know that he was terrified of some future infant because of some predictions, they might laugh at him, which would be even worse! Nothing terrifies a tyrant more than ridicule and he shuddered at the prospect. And, of course astrologers went wrong as often back then, as they do now, so all the hassle might not really be necessary after all. Kansa obviously had a real dilemma on his hands."

"Then what was the way out?" DK was curious

"Oddly enough, it looks like the solution came from Vasudev. Vasudev was worried that Kansa might indeed kill his new bride. Therefore, it was he who suggested that there was no need to kill Devaki, if Kansa kept them under strict guard. This suited Kansa too, so he kept his sister and brother-in-law under house arrest with only very few trusted people in the know. Descriptions of dungeons or dark cells look most fanciful. Where was the need? As long as his sister and brother-in-law were in accommodation befitting their royal standing under trusted, watchful eyes, it was enough. They would be mere 'guests' for public consumption and would not merit much discussion," JT pointed out.

"This is beginning to sound a little more reasonable. What happened next?" DK wanted to know.

"In due course, Devaki had a son and Vasudev informed Kansa about it. Now here is a dilemma many writers have wrestled with. If the prophesy was that the eighth child was to kill Kansa, where was the need to kill the first seven? The standard explanation has been to bring Narada or some other divine element into it with some glib logic as to how in a 'wheel' it is difficult to say which is the first spoke and which is the last and so on."

"What could a more plausible reason then be?" DK wondered.

JT explained patiently. "There is a very plausible explanation based on what you and I already know of the psyche of tyrants and their desperation to control narratives. Kansa wanted his subjects to know as little as possible. Of what use would these seven siblings of the potentially dangerous one be to him? Alive, they could have been a source of embarrassment; it would after all have been difficult even for a tyrant to stop babies from crying or falling ill or injuring themselves, necessitating servants and wet nurses and *vaidyas* and others to attend to them. Keeping the whole enterprise secret would have been be so much tougher. Much simpler would be to have them killed quietly; may be spread stories of a miscarriage. Surely, he had enough henchmen to do the job."

"Yes, I guess there was no real need for Amrish Puri style 'Ha Ha Hu Hu'. And Devaki and Vasudev would have had no option but to keep quiet since they would have been secretly praying for the prophesy to be true and pinning their hopes on the eighth child for deliverance from their hell. It is beginning to make sense. So what happened next?" DK asked.

"You know, people fall into patterns of behaviour easily. So did Kansa and Vasudev as time went by. Kansa had, of course, kept guards but Vasudev himself would inform Kansa about the birth of a child and Kansa would lose no time in eliminating it. After the fourth child was dealt with, Kansa patted himself on the back; it was all too easy really, he had got scared needlessly. He had started trusting Vasudev too, because he had been prompt with his communications. So Kansa relaxed the terms of their house arrest, allowing Vasudev to move out. After all Vasudev's fiefdom was just across the Yamuna river, taxes and tributes still needed to be collected. He could be brought in anytime if needed. Therefore, Kansa could see no merit in holding onto him any longer."

"So Devaki was pretty much left alone with a couple of attendants and guards while Vasudev could come and go as he pleased?"

"Exactly," remarked JT. "But Vasudev did much more than that, on both sides of the Yamuna, in fact. As I said earlier, in Mathura there was much disenchantment with Kansa in his court. In particular, his Prime Minister Anart and Acharya Gargacharya were most dissatisfied. Vasudev had known them earlier and took full advantage of his new found freedom to forge stronger bonds with them."

"Sounds logical. But you said both sides of the Yamuna?"

"Yes. About 10 km or six miles from Mathura, on the other side of Yamuna, was the village of Gokul. The chief there was Vasudev's younger cousin and dear friend Nanda. In fact so close were they that Vasudev's first wife Rohini was staying with Nanda, while Vasudev was under house arrest in Mathura. Incidentally, he had several wives, Rohini was the first and Devaki the last."

DK interjected. "But wasn't Rohini the mother of Balaram?"

"Yes! Vasudev clearly took advantage of his furlough to visit Nanda, with whom Rohini was staying. Her son Balaram was born around the same time as Devaki's sixth child. Do your maths! Vasudev also took Nanda into confidence about the prophesy and other matters."

DK thought it over for a few minutes. "How different the story sounds when details are filled in. Please continue."

"In due course, Nanda's wife Yashoda got pregnant and soon Devaki also conceived for the eighth time. Do note the sequence. It could well have been planned that way by the fathers, we will never know. By this time, Vasudev had completely turned Prime Minister Anart and Acharya Gargacharya to his side. He had also quietly arranged for Nanda to move to a convenient location just across the Yamuna," JT explained patiently.

"Yes, I was thinking that 10 kms would be quite a distance for what is to follow after a tiring river crossing."

"Vasudev had of course figured it all out. It had taken him a lot of effort to persuade Nanda to do his part in what was to follow, but then Nanda was also keen on getting rid of the tyrannical Kansa. Plus he was to get a very capable 'son' if all went according to plan and the prophesy came true."

"Yes, the pieces have started falling into place. Go on, please," DK persisted.

"The rest is not too difficult to figure out. At the right time, Nanda acquired a temporary accommodation right across the river from Mathura. When Yashoda's child, a girl, was born there, Nanda ensured that the mother and child were kept separate under some pretext. Soon Devaki delivered a baby boy, in fact a little premature, so Kansa was not fully alert. The guards had already been suborned by Prime Minister Anart and Acharya Gargacharya by then and a well-padded cane basket had been kept ready. Vasudev swam across the flooded Yamuna on the rainy night we all know about, and exchanged the babies as planned with Nanda. Devaki was still unconscious when he returned, so neither of the ladies was any wiser."

"And next morning Kansa was informed as per the set pattern and he murdered the child. What a horrible man. I suppose, Nanda, his wife and the child moved back quietly to Gokul in the next few days."

"Exactly. And Gokul celebrated the birth of a son to its chieftain," said JT.

"Hmm... you have opened my eyes to looking at things in a completely new way. My eyes seem to have been shut in other ways too, for we have passed Pune where we were supposed to have our lunch break. But this Joshi Lunch Home looks hygienic enough and it seem to have ample parking too."

JT smiled. "Yes, lunch would be a good idea. I am hungry and thirsty too."

***

"There weren't too many people wearing masks out there in the restaurant," DK remarked, a few minutes after the *nandighosh* resumed its journey.

"Yes," agreed JT. "People do have a tendency to believe that the worst will happen to somebody else, not to them. It has always been so." He swung *nandighosh* effortlessly on to the highway. He had taken the wheel after lunch and seemed to handle it with utmost ease.

"Did that happen to Kansa too? At least after he had dealt with Devaki's first two or three babies?"

"It may well have happened. Times may have changed but basic human nature probably hasn't."

"So tell me, where exactly did you read all these alternate explanations? They sound reasonable enough." DK was curious.

"There are many ancient texts which talk of Krishna. Mahabharat, or Jaya as it was known first, was composed originally around 3000 BC with some 8,800 *shlokas*, later expanded to a lakh of them. Then came many others, prominent being Harivansa Purana composed around 200 BC and Vishnu Purana around the same time. Some others like Shatapatha Brahmana, Padma Purana, Kurma Purana were written at various times from 900 BC to 200 BC. These were all written by scholars but other than Mahabharat, all were clearly written at least hundred, more likely thousands of years after the birth of Krishna with plenty of subsequent additions and alterations."

DK was thoughtful. "Anything written after such a long passage of time is bound to have ambiguities and variations in different accounts. After all, news reports today from different sources can't even agree on how many Covid cases were found in the country yesterday! So how does one figure out what was the most likely thing to have happened?"

"That could be the reason why scholars and wise people may have used the device of divinity which is adequate for the common man, just as governments use people's trust and unquestioning attitude while releasing Covid numbers. Both work well most of the time. But for the more inquisitive and discerning, a little more effort is required. Cross checking of sources, dates and use of intelligence can lead to a pretty good idea of what might actually have happened."

"So Jaya or Mahabharat was the first to refer to Krishna?"

JT clarified patiently. "Yes, but remember there is a long history of oral story telling in India. And it would not be correct to downplay something only because written sources are hard to find. Krishna hardly has any real role in Mahabharat till at least his move to Dwarka which happened after he was well out of his teens. Thereafter, of course, he dominates the proceedings in many ways."

"I understand. Let us get back to where he has the main role, his early childhood...where we had left him before lunch. Yes, we now have a young Krishna growing up in Gokul. I have a number of questions about his childhood and some incidents that supposedly took place then..."

"Before that I have some questions too," said JT with a smile.

"For me?" DK was surprised.

"Yes, of course. You have heard of Abhimanyu Mishra, the Indian boy from New Jersey who became the youngest chess grandmaster at age 12?"

"I seem to remember having read something like that," said DK.

"And do you know at what age did Mozart compose his first symphony?"

"No."

"9 years."

"The point you are trying to making is..." DK enquired.

"My point is that child prodigies are not an unknown phenomenon. Music, chess and mathematics are where they seem to show up early. But they are everywhere, from Spelling Bee contests in USA to even our own talent contests on TV."

"Yes, some of the performances are truly amazing."

"Everything points to the likelihood that Krishna was a hugely talented prodigy. For his fame to have lasted for thousands of years, he was not only born as an exceptionally gifted prodigy in one area as most prodigies are, but a 360 degree one; moreover, he also seems to have been exceptionally perceptive and a quick learner."

"I get where you are coming from. Once we factor in that premise, understanding and accepting child Krishna's achievements will become easier."

JT smiled. "Exactly. So let us see how Krishna's early days and years in Gokul would have been like. As a cute, cuddly young child growing up, there would have been no shortage of doting gopis around. Why, even today, any young mother just has to walk into a group of young school or college girls with her baby and all of them start coochie cooing in no time. It is a very natural phenomenon. So we have this young, handsome, smart, extremely intelligent baby boy growing up amidst all these young doting gopas and gopis in Gokul. The prodigy soon has a big fan following among the locals because of his rare talents and intelligence."

"What about his flute playing?" DK asked.

"That Krishna was a child prodigy, we have already accepted and there seems to be some symbiotic relationship between music and child prodigies."

"Yes," said DK. "The ages of contestants with astonishing skills seems to keep going lower every year in all these Little Champs type shows."

JT smiled. "Yes, they might have to rename them as 'Baby Champs!' Even so there are quite a few references to Krishna and Balaram being taught music and wrestling by Acharya Shrutiketu and Sandeepani Rishi when he visited them during their stay in Vrindavan and later on too. What seems beyond doubt though is that at a very early age Krishna acquired mastery over the flute."

"I used to play the guitar in school and I am familiar with the advantages that playing a musical instrument has while dealing with girls at that age," DK reminisced with a smile as if tickled by some memory.

"And it has been scientifically established now that cows respond very favourably to music. There are many professionally run dairies in the country which have gentle music playing most of the time in their cattle sheds and stables."

"I was about to ask about their migration to Vrindavan. But before that should we take all of Bal Krishna's early exploits in Gokul, fondness for *dahi*, the *maakhan chori*, the fun with all his cow herd friends as all being true?"

"Even allowing for some exaggeration by writers, these seem harmless enough and there should be no problem accepting these at face value."

"What about accounts of what seem miraculous exploits? The Kaliya Naag, the taming of or controlling of a wild horse or a raging bull? How do we explain a child accomplishing all these?" DK demanded.

"Most of these episodes are supposed to be from his Vrindavan days. However, it hardly matters in which order we consider them. Yes, these are a little more challenging, but thank goodness we are in the 21st century and thank god for YouTube."

"I don't understand."

"Try searching for Bull Fighting or Rodeos on YouTube some time. Some of the chaps tackling monstrous bulls or grumpy horses are a little bigger than regular 10 or 12-year-olds in Spain or Mexico or USA. Great reflexes, wonderful hand-eye-feet coordination and swift movements are in any case cherished skills in every village *akhara* in the world from time immemorial. They seem to work well for defeating big animals too. There is no reason to suppose that young Indian stalwarts did not possess these skills in ancient times or do not possess them now."

"True, seeing is believing and now that you mention it, I do remember seeing young bull fighters taming big bulls. In fact, we can see some of these skills in our own Jallikattu videos which surface every year," agreed DK. "Okay, so the miracles may not have been so miraculous after all, just outstanding feats of someone extremely gifted. Let us then talk of the larger issues of the community's migration to Vrindavan in which Krishna is supposed to have played a leading role. Quite unbelievable for a child so young."

"Fair enough. Have you noticed one thing?" JT asked, "The truly gifted ones or the prodigies end up becoming the focal points of their families, then of their communities and so on as they grow in stature?"

"Like who?"

"Check out *The Queen's Gambit* or any of the dozen movies on prodigies now available on various OTT platforms. Once their talent starts getting recognised, their lives and the lives of their close ones — parents, siblings and so on — start revolving around them. Schools give them extra leaves whenever they want, in fact even re-schedule the exam time-tables if needed. Their voices start becoming more important in family decision making and all related matters."

"You mean to say that is what happened with Krishna?" DK asked.

"It happens even when the prodigy has no other talent. In Krishna's case, everything points to the fact that apart from being gifted, he had exceptional intelligence and leadership qualities too. He organised gopalas on a few curd mischief missions and so on...it would have been a wonder if the opinion of a boy with such attributes had not been sought on any important decision. It is also entirely possible that he noticed the need first."

"So what prompted the community to shift to Vrindavan?"

"The grass around Gokul had started to dry up. This is something that communities which live on cattle grazing and breeding have to adapt to everywhere. Hence the cowherds, the gopalas, had to go further and further in search of food for the cattle. The distances over which they needed to carry back fruits, flowers and firewood had started becoming longer. And of course the cattle could not have been in the best of condition given the long distances they needed to travel every day."

"And Krishna noticed it?"

"Some others may have noticed it too, but it would have been a wonder if Krishna had not noticed it. Moreover, an instinctive leader is never satisfied with identifying a problem, his nature compels him to seek a solution."

"So Krishna suggested the move from Gokul to Vrindavan?"

JT shrugged. "More likely it was one of the elders who would have been more familiar with the geography who brought up Vrindavan. However, identifying the need for a change of location and articulating it was probably Krishna's doing."

DK looked out of the window. It had been getting dark for a little while, Satara's lights had begun to appear bright.

"There is so much more I want to know even about Krishna's early days. About Vrindavan, about Radha, holding up the Govardhan *parvat* and most of all about the move back to

Mathura for his face off with Kansa... but I think we better leave these for tomorrow. Very soon it will be time for me to talk to Neeta. I had promised her that I will not miss my walks so I better turn in soon and wake up early."

"Makes sense. This petrol pump and food court look perfect for our first night halt. Looks a big parking lot too." JT brought *nandighosh* to a gentle stop.

DK opened the door. "Let me first have a word with the boys at the petrol pump and organise the filling-up and cleaning up for tomorrow morning."

❑❑❑

CHAPTER 2

Growing Up

"India may not have great trailer parks like the USA, but we do have one advantage. We have willing and capable hands everywhere. A modest tip and in an hour, *nandighosh* is as good as new, washrooms cleaned, all the dust and grime of yesterday wiped off," said DK as he looked with pride at the handiwork of the local *Chotu*. The duo had just finished their breakfast and were getting ready to leave Satara behind.

"Let me take the wheel DK."

"Sure" replied DK, secretly relieved since JT drove like a master while he was a bit wary of the narrower countryside roads with undisciplined traffic. The countryside seemed to be largely oblivious of Covid.

"Let us head towards Belgaum, we will take a lunch break at any convenient stop around 1 o' clock."

"Perfect!"

"Here, have this *Kandi pedha*. I picked it up on my morning walk."

"How was the walk?" JT inquired politely, taking a small *pedha*.

DK remembered. He had woken up at 4 am with a start. He had dreamt of being enveloped by a fog and he was groping to find his way... and then he was awake. Not scary but unusual. It was too early for a walk and he had dozed around till suddenly it was 6 am. He had quickly got ready and started out on his morning walk.

"Very pleasant actually, the roads are very clean. I saw a tiny shop open and asked the owner about famous places around here. He talked of the palace and how a few centuries back a local Mahabharat had taken place in the area about succession dispute among family members of the Maratha empire. Fortunately this one was not settled on a battlefield, though splitting up between Kolhapur and Satara surely weakened the Maratha power. Interesting how Mahabharat references slip into our daily conversations everywhere."

"Yes, the epics are part of our national DNA," agreed JT.

"The man sold me some *Kandi pedhas*. Made of *khoya* and *elaichi* or cardamom. Largely proteins so can't be too bad for my sugar though it is slightly sweet. This entire stretch up to Belgaum is famous for it and Neeta told me yesterday to give it a try. Of course, she also asked me to get a *Kashida* sari from Belgaum. Tell me JT, how do women always seem to know what things a place is famous for?"

JT laughed. "They understood the importance of social networking long before Mark Zuckerberg was born!"

DK laughed. "Talking of women, where exactly does Radha stand in Krishna's life?"

JT became serious, though the twinkle in his eyes stayed.

"That is an interesting question. Before we talk of Radha, tell me what do you know of her?"

"Only what everyone in India seems to know. That she was someone Krishna was close to during his Vrindavan days. Many versions say more than close. There are some very colourful descriptions of their togetherness. There are many Radha-Krishna temples, in fact more than any of Krishna alone, leave aside any with his wives like Rukmini or Satyabhama."

"Let me ask you a follow-up question. What is it about this that bothers you?"

"Frankly, the thought that someone regarded as an 'incarnation' should be thought to have indulged in some of the activities described does trouble me. The two images don't seem to be compatible." The pain in DK's voice was discernible.

"Okay, let us talk of Radha first," said JT. "There is no mention of Radha in the *puranas* like Harivansa Purana or Vishnu Purana. Radha is first mentioned in literature only about 1000 years ago but attention started focussing on her only after the poet Jaydev wrote his Geet Govind in the 13th century. It spoke of transcendental love between Radha and Krishna in Vrindavan."

"I never knew that! That would make it about 4000 years after Krishna and Mahabharat era!"

"Yes, give or take a few hundred years at least. But let us leave that aside for a moment. It is after all possible for something to be generally true even if it came to us through the oral rendition tradition rather than the written down one."

DK interjected. "Yes, in fact I did read that King Parikshit, grandson of Arjun had also brought up a similar query and the answer he got from the *rishis* was that since Krishna was an *avataar* of god and protector of Dharma, he himself was exempt from its observance. Not very satisfactory but yes, the oral rendition tradition was certainly there."

"Which is why one needs a little caution in treating sensitive matters that may have come down orally for a long time before someone wrote it all down. Okay, let us get back to Radha."

"I am all ears," said DK.

"There are two ways to look at it. First, that Radha was an entirely fictional character created by writers, maybe even before Jaydev. He was the most prominent writer to use her as a peg to imagine what an adolescent Krishna might have been like. Krishna-Radha relationship has been described by so many of them, has such a wide variation, it ranges from innocent love to all possible shades of *shringaar ras*. Thus Radha being a fictional character seems to be the most likely scenario given that the name was mentioned in literature after such a long gap. Do you find anything wrong with it?"

"I am not sure if I am comfortable with the image of Krishna being used by writers in a *rasleela* kind of imagery," said DK.

"Have you thought about the possibility that the problem may be with your conditioning rather than the imagery itself? After all India is a land where an uninhibited treatise on love making like Kamasutra was written, where even today there are countless carvings on any number of temples depicting our deities in every conceivable position? Could it be that over-sensitivity to the subject, which entered this land only around the 12th or 13th century, possibly coinciding with the advent of travellers from the West, may be influencing our responses?"

"Now that is a thought which has never entered my mind," conceded DK.

"Bear in mind that there is hardly any prudery about matters of intimacy in most countries east of India."

"Okay, I will think about it. But you had mentioned two possibilities?" said DK.

"Yes, the second possibility is that Radha did exist even though early narrations about her were only oral. In which case, we need to take stories about her a little more seriously," JT explained with clarity as always.

"Yes, I want to know more about it."

"The commonest account refers to Radha, as a married woman who had returned to Vrindavan, to her mother's place after disagreements with her husband."

"Yes, yes, that is the one I have read!" DK nodded in agreement.

"Most of those versions say that Radha was about 22 and Krishna around 13-14 when they met."

"Exactly!"

"In that case wouldn't it be more like Rishi Kapoor falling in love with his teacher in the film *Mera Naam Joker*? Most people go through puppy love or infatuation as it is called. So how is it a big deal if Krishna, whether he was a super high IQ gifted prodigy or an incarnate bound by laws of flesh, also went through it? Thank goodness our ancients never sought exemptions for our gods from *shareer-dharma* or functions of the body the way North Korean Kim has done! Is a case of puppy love worth so much fuss?"

"But what about all the *rasleelas* which have entered the public discourse?"

"Yes, there are many of them," conceded JT "but it would be foolish to think of the imagery purely in physical terms. Some have been depicted aesthetically and have differing interpretations.

For example, one interpretation is that Krishna's *rasleela* with the gopis is not an ordinary dance on a small scale. It actually represents the universal dance of creation which has been going on for eternity. It symbolises the everlasting drama of the making and unmaking of the universe. It gives you a glimpse of that divine dance and that immense cosmic orchestra. If that be so, Krishna's *maha-raas* ceases to have a sexual connotation."

DK was mystified. "Then what is Krishna's dance about and what does it signify?"

JT smiled. "Another interpretation is that Krishna does not dance as just Krishna, he represents the whole of the male element in creation, known in Sanskrit as *purusha*. And similarly the gopis represent the entire female element, *prakriti*. The *maha-raas* represents the combined dance of *prakriti* and *purusha* which make creation itself possible. Again, this is a metaphorical representation and ought not to be interpreted literally."

DK marvelled at the explanation and the clarity of it all. Why did I not think of it myself? "But what about some of the extreme interpretations with emphasis just on the sexuality?"

"Sure, some people do take advantage of our traditions of giving space to every opinion. We have a marvellous tradition where our scholars and *rishis* have discussed and debated even existence of god. We have given space to even our arch villains.

In India you can find temples devoted to Ravan and Duryodhan also. Why should we get perturbed if a few writers use that liberty to titillate their readers? Very easy to ignore them."

"How simple and logical you make it sound!" DK exclaimed.

"It is really very simple and it actually has little to do with Krishna's divinity issue, except in a tangential way — if it did happen, with Radha or some other *gopi*, it was all a part of Krishna's growing up. He was like a sponge, absorbing every lesson and storing it for some future use."

"We spoke of Krishna's *shareer-dharma* and I am now reminded of my stomach-dharma because of its constant growling. Let us take a break here at this Belgaum Kitchen and enjoy some *Bisibelebhaath*."

"Sure, always ready to re-fuel," said JT with a smile.

***

"Why does food at highway stops and roadside *dhabas* always taste so good?" said DK, trying to keep awake as they resumed their journey after lunch. A few months of retirement and staying locked-in at home has got me used to power naps, he thought. Neeta won't believe that someone who worked 12 hours a day most of his life, is dozing off after eating a plate of *Bisibelebhaath*!

"I guess it is because of the freshness of the vegetables and other supplies. Also, since shelf life is not much of a concern, most supplies would be free of pesticides or preservatives," said JT. "Food wastage is such a problem. An estimated 40 per cent of all of India's food production goes waste."

DK wanted to get back to his main interest. "Okay, let us return to Krishna. So far it seems to be clear that we can reach up to Krishna's adolescence without bringing any divinity into it and also, even in the stories involving Radha, true or false, there is nothing that really needs to trouble us. But what about the next stage? What about Krishna's holding up the Govardhan mountain on his fingertip? Wasn't that a miraculous act requiring strength beyond a human being, even a super human being?" asked DK.

JT laughed. "Funny you brought it up just after we discussed agricultural produce waste."

"What do you mean?"

"Let us rewind from Govardhan mountain bit and try and understand the context. It was all about Indra Puja."

"Yes, I have read about that. But in India there have always been *pujas* of so many types."

"True, and India is not the only one. Agricultural societies have always placed a premium on rains, so it is no surprise that people started 'praying' to some sort of a rain god from very early on."

"Sure, logical enough."

"That part is fine, but then came ritual offerings. Over a period of time, these ritual offerings tended to grow. So many *seers* of ghee, so many *maunds* of rice, vegetables, milk, honey, everything was welcome as a 'sacrifice' to propitiate an unknown Deva, Indra Deva, the god of rains."

"I can see that the *puja* scale would go up with time, seems to happen in the contemporary period as well."

"Beyond a point, all these represent an increasing burden on the resources of the small communities, villages and so on."

"And people would find it tough to say no because of the burden of tradition and peer pressure of what will people say." DK drew upon his experience of dealing with people coming around for donations for some *puja* or the other.

"Exactly. Except the young spirited Krishna. Understand the situation. Here is a young lad of maybe 14-15, prodigiously gifted in many areas, highly intelligent, confronted with what seemed to him to be a patently unjust and irrational system of burdening everyone in the community, rich or poor."

"And he had no baggage of tradition to uphold, he was not old enough for that."

"Yes. There is an interesting proverb about this stage of life, in effect saying that 'moustaches and opinions start sprouting at about the same age'."

"Ha Ha Ha! I used to have arguments daily with my father as a teenager," DK reminisced.

"So Indra Puja was a perfect target for the young Krishna. Moreover, he was the leader of the boys of his generation in Vrindavan, all the gopals. He called all of them together, told them about his opposition to an Indra Puja which would mean enormous wastage of precious food, representing days and months of hard work for all the villagers. He wanted that the practice to be stopped forthwith."

"Did the boys agree or did some of them have reservations?"

"Some of the older ones had reservations, the hold of tradition is strong. But here's the thing. Weather cycles were among the first things that Man had mastered on planet earth. Even in those days they knew very well about water evaporating or the convection process, cloud formation leading to rains and so on. They understood seasons very well. Why, forget human beings, these things are so elementary that birds, animals all understood them early on and factored them into their migratory patterns."

"Yes, I have seen videos of birds and wildebeest on National Geographic and Discovery channels," agreed DK.

"As to our ancestors, they had understood even complex stuff like planetary movements long before Krishna was born. So it is not as if the gopals were unaware of the weather cycles and the general predictability of the rainy season. When Krishna asked them pointedly as to where Indra Dev fitted into all this, they were forced to question the practice of Indra Puja and consider joining Krishna's rebellion, for that is what it was, an intelligent youngster's rebellion against a tradition."

"So did they join him?"

"Yes, they did. Once they were on board, he led them all to the village elders and announced the decision to stop Indra Puja. The village elders were practically presented with a *fait accompli*, for of course, it was the boys who were required by custom to collect all the firewood and other *puja* paraphernalia." explained JT.

"Okay, so the *puja* was abandoned," said DK.

"Yes, but we need to understand the larger context here too. By then, young Krishna's name had started to be known in the neighbouring areas. Indra Puja was a widespread practice, not restricted just to Vrindavan and neighbouring areas. People all over started following developments in Vrindavan closely. There were many who feared Indra Dev's wrath and were sure a terrible fate awaited Vrindavan whose inhabitants had let a young upstart talk them into abandoning a long standing practice."

"Then what happened?" By now DK was engrossed in the narrative.

"That particular day it started to rain heavily and the downpour continued for a few days. Many residents of Vrindavan were petrified but Krishna remained undaunted. On to Govardhan mountain, he said. He and his boys helped the women, children, old and infirm across the mountain where they sheltered in a few of the many caves there. What followed was fairly predictable; we know what happens in case of such a deluge or even a cloudburst, we see it happening every year in some part of India or the other."

"The waters recede after a few days," said DK. He had seen this sequence play out year after year in Mumbai.

"Exactly. The waters receded and in a few days Vrindavan was back to normal."

"So that was the end of that story?"

“Not so fast. Two things happened and both are very important. First, the entire incident, people’s fright and fear of the unknown probably led Krishna to believe that some form of *puja* was essential to keep up their morale. So he suggested a Govardhan Puja, since it was that mountain which had offered them shelter when needed. More than the *puja* itself, it shows a mind quick to absorb lessons about human nature and take action on it.”

“And the second?”

“The second was that word about Krishna started spreading beyond Vrindavan, to places like Mathura and other towns nearby. Don’t forget India by then had a well-developed communications network of traditional travellers like monks and mendicants, craftsmen and traders. Obviously stories of valour and heroism always grow in repetition. In no time at all, the story had become that a young boy, Krishna, had raised Govardhan mountain on his fingertips, defied Indra Dev and had come out victorious.”

“Now that you have explained it, it all seems very logical. Obviously if he had defeated ‘Indra Dev’, he must be divine himself — that is how common people must have interpreted it!”

“Bull’s eye. That could have been the beginning of people believing that Krishna might be an *avataar* himself.”

“Never realised how quickly the afternoon has passed. Let us call it a day here and celebrate Krishna’s victory over Indra Dev,” said DK. He wanted to soak in all that he had heard.

“We will stop here alright but any celebrations might be premature. For one pair of ears which heard stories of young Krishna’s exploits belonged to Kansa. He was in no mood to listen about *avataars* and began his terrifying counter plans immediately. But let us leave them for tomorrow.”

❑❑❑

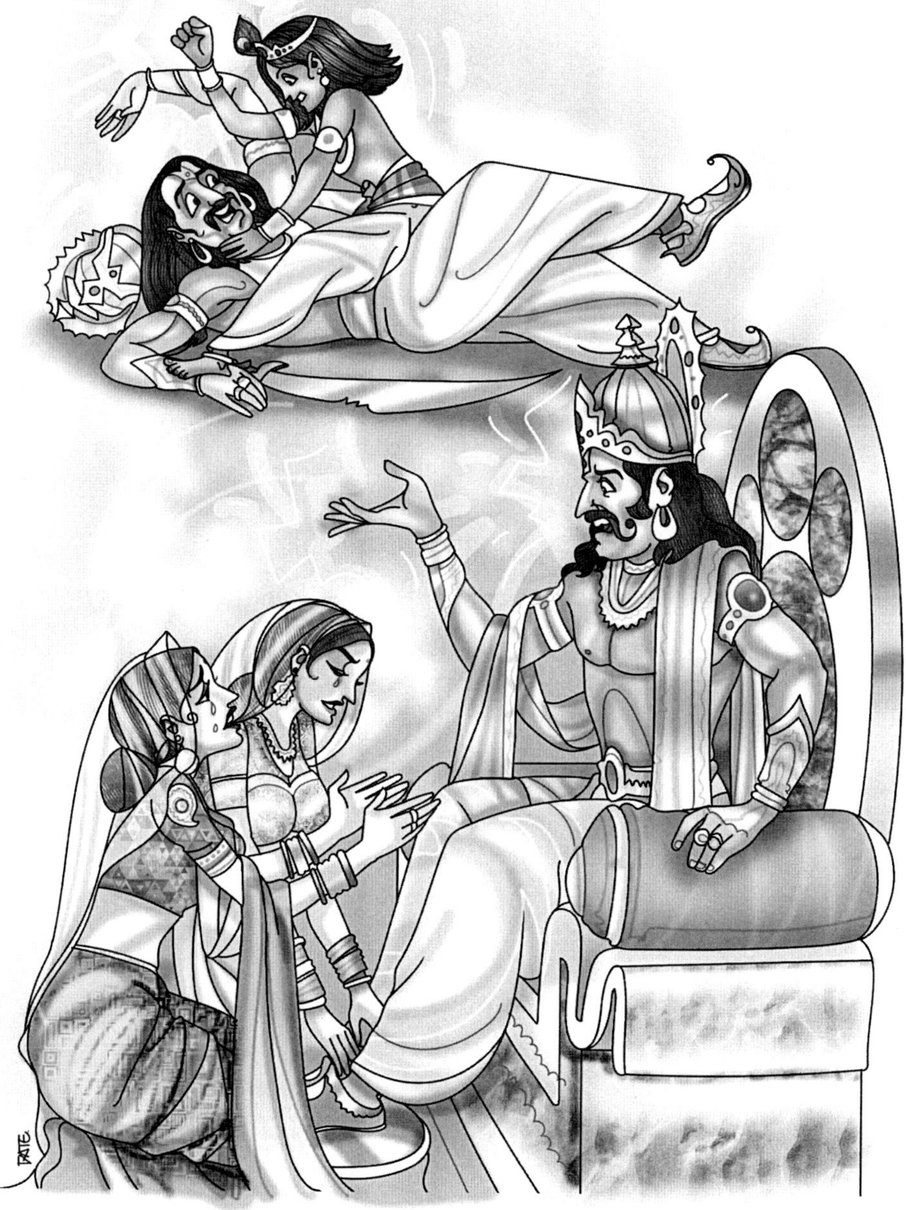

CHAPTER 3

Coming of Age

"Not slept too well DK?" asked JT as *nandighosh* hit the highway again on day three of the journey.

"The man who was to deliver the Kashida saris came late yesterday. We got talking and I was reminded of what you said, that in India we have a tradition of offering space to everyone, including our villains."

"Yes, I did say that. What happened?"

"Did you know that there is an Ashwatthama temple around here? With the strangest of customs. A day after Holi, people do a *lotangan,* or rolling while lying completely prostrate on the ground, at this temple to thank him for having granted their wishes! Rest of the year it is deserted."

"Ha Ha. Yes, Ashwatthama would make it to any villains' gallery of our history. We can add getting you to wake up late to his list of sins."

"No no, I got up in time alright," DK remembered getting up with the same dream at 5 early morning. He had promised Neeta he would check his BP and sugar levels regularly, so he had checked them. At 135/90 and 110, the levels were better than when he had last checked in Mumbai. Very pleased even though he was slightly short of sleep, DK had got ready and stepped out for his morning walk. The fresh air had felt so good. But the eyes did have the tell-tale reddishness which JT had spotted.

"And how were the saris? Were they approved?" asked JT. "And how are things there in USA?"

"Thankfully, they were approved quickly by Neeta. Things are a bit stressful there though. Doctors said something about fluid being less, head position and so on which I did not fully understand."

"No point stressing about things which are not in your control."

"True, that is why I find our discussion so useful. It helps clear my doubts and distracts me from my worries," said DK.

"So where were we?" asked JT.

"Yes, Krishna's achievements, especially in getting Indra Puja abandoned had reached Kansa's ears and he started plotting. There is much about the sequencing of that part, of whatever I have read, about Kansa's activities that has puzzled me. Many versions talk of Kansa having deployed his agents, Putna or some demons to kill Krishna earlier."

"Those were probably fanciful insertions by writers trying to enhance Krishna's valour in order to justify some form of divinity."

"What about the *Akashvani* that told Kansa, when he killed the girl child substituted for Krishna, that his nemesis was already born?"

"Same answer, likely introduction to justify Krishna's divinity. As evidence, just look at the unfolding of events: if indeed there had been such an *Akashvan*i, the first person suspected of subterfuge, of spiriting away a new born boy, would have been Vasudev. Was any action taken against him?"

"No, but Vasudev being his brother-in-law, Kansa may have hesitated to kill him or even take action against him!" DK persisted.

"Possible, but Kansa would surely have deduced that Vasudev could not have done anything without accomplices. The guards would have been in chains immediately and Kansa would have got them to spill the beans on their masters before you could have said 'Tyrant'. Did the guards get arrested?

No. Did the PM Anart or Gargacharya get arrested? No. As Sherlock Holmes would say, why did the dog not bark? It is quite elementary DK."

"You mean to say Kansa suspected nothing?" DK wondered.

"Not for a while at least. Vasudev and Devaki continued living in Mathura; in fact after a while all controls on their movements seem to have been eased, further proof that Kansa had relaxed. There are versions that Vasudev and Devaki visited Gokul, where Vasudev and Nanda shared the secret of Krishna's birth with the two ladies, Devaki and Yashoda, and young Krishna himself. They of course urged utmost secrecy since security was still an issue."

"Okay, let us get back to Vrindavan and Mathura after the Govardhan mountain part. What about the wrestling match? How did that come about?"

"It is possible that the overcoming of a bull by a young lad may have come to Kansa's notice. But he probably sat up and got alarmed about happenings in Vrindavan only after Indra Puja and Govardhan mountain episode. Exaggerated stories of how a youngster had led the people there to safety after getting the Indra Puja abandoned, how he 'lifted the mountain on his little finger' surely reached Kansa and like all tyrants, he had a good antenna for any threat to his rule. It might even be that whispers of Krishna being a divine incarnation, that probably started circulating around this time, also reached him."

"Did he connect it to the events of 16-17 years ago? The prophesies, for example?" asked DK.

"Looks very doubtful because no action was taken against possible suspects even at this stage, which surely would have happened if indeed Kansa's suspicions about events that long ago had been aroused."

"So what was his plan?"

"He plotted carefully. He was smart enough to figure that the lads — for by now Krishna and Balaram had acquired the reputation of being an awesome twosome — would be enormously popular locally, so they would have to be drawn away from their home ground. And to allay any suspicions that the two were specifically being targeted, he arranged a wrestling tournament, inviting wrestlers from far and near. He invited princes and princesses from neighbouring areas too."

"But didn't Nanda and other seniors smell a rat when Krishna-Balaram were invited?" DK persisted.

"Come on, give Kansa some credit. He sent a personal emissary, Akrur, to meet Nanda. Now Akrur was a high ranking Yadav, too senior for a village headman like Nanda to say no to. But Akrur was smart too. He hedged his bets by inviting Krishna-Balaram to stay at his house, away from the palace; he had already told Kansa his plan to do so with the perfectly valid reason that young cowherds, stepping out of their small bubbles for the first time, might get overwhelmed at the mention of staying at a palace, which was Kansa's original intention. You didn't get to become a senior Yadav functionary for nothing."

"I can visualise the scene," said DK. "Nanda and Krishna-Balaram were trapped."

"Yes they were. And before they left for Mathura, the two young lads, perhaps 16-19 year old, were duly cautioned by Nanda."

"But the versions I have read put Krishna's age as less than 11 when he went to Mathura!"

"Kansa would have made a laughing stock of himself if he had invited some 10-12 year olds to Mathura for a wrestling tournament. He was a tyrant but surely he was not that stupid."

"But then why are there so many versions saying authoritatively that Krishna was less than 11 years old when he went from Vrindavan to Mathura?" DK wanted to know.

"Yes, there are many versions suggesting Krishna was less than 11 and practically all of them are from sources who had waxed lyrical about Krishna, Radha and the gopis. The problem for those who talk of Krishna being less than 11 is that if they make him a little older, they will need to accept that it was not an innocent child who had left Vrindavan, but someone who may have had a brush with puppy love, with perhaps some physical overtones too. In order to avoid facing that, those versions suggest the prima facie absurd possibility of a 10 or 11 year old defeating a trained wrestler. And to overcome that logical flaw, a divine angle seems to have been introduced," pointed out JT.

"And you don't find that acceptable?" DK asked.

"It is not that. Not at all. My point is that once a divine angle is introduced, why 10 or 11, even a 5 year old can be said to have killed giants. Once divinity is factored in, there is no need for any further discussion. What we are trying to do, as we decided right at the beginning of our journey, is to see if an alternate explanation can be found for the events described without taking recourse to the supposed divine origins of Krishna. From what I can see, we have been able to find reasonable alternate explanations for everything so far, till the point of Krishna-Balaram heading to Mathura as mid-to-late teenagers."

"But we may get stuck now I think. How can two youngsters, no matter how strong they are physically, take on a king with all his guards and army, not to mention the two famous wrestlers, Chanoor and Mushtik? I can't see how this could have been possible, unless there was a divine hand involved!" DK was not one to give up easily.

"Ha Ha. Let us examine the full context first. Krishna and Balaram arrived in Mathura a few days before the contest was to take place. Mathura was a big town of the day and the two country boys wandered around the town, all wide eyed for the next few days. Such wide roads, such well-stocked shops and items for sale like fine silk which the boys had probably not even heard of till then. But as Krishna absorbed all these, he also picked up undertones of resentment among the people."

"What do you mean?" DK wanted to know.

"We already know that Krishna was an extremely fast learner. And here there were many people who recognised him as the hero of the Indra Puja and Govardhan mountain story. They would have been comfortable in hinting about or sharing their unease about the local ruling dispensation with him. Krishna's political antenna was obviously extraordinary and he probably felt completely at home on this large stage. He realised very early on that the key to defeating a tyrant was getting some public support. He absorbed who were the important people in the court and what issues resonated with the people," said JT.

"Now that you mention it, I seem to remember a story about Kubja, a woman with a hunchback, whom Krishna helped out."

"There was another one of the dead body of a bow-maker being found with people suspecting the involvement of the palace. The details really don't matter too much, what matters is that young Krishna took to politics like a duck takes to water. He knew what the chink in the enemy's armour was, public opinion, and went about exploiting it like a master."

"Then what happened at the wrestling bout?" DK wanted to know.

"When the match-up of the best wrestlers of the day, Chanoor and Mushtik was announced with Krishna and Balaram, the public sensed what was happening, the entire gallery booed and whistled. It is difficult to fool people all the time and once people lose their fear, the tyrants begin to cower."

"Did Chanoor and Mushtik lose their nerves because of the crowd's reaction?" DK wondered.

"Could be. But it is not inconceivable for strong lads of 16-19 to thrash ageing senior pros who could have got overconfident over time. Happens all the time in sports. Recall Sachin Tendulkar taking on a Waqar Younis or even a young 18-year-old Cassius Clay thrashing older, bigger boxers like Sonny Liston early in his career. 'Move like a butterfly, sting like a bee' was his tagline. The point I want to make is that there is no need to bring in divinity, if speed and skill that a once-in-a-millennia prodigy might possess can explain it."

DK nodded. "Yes, it is possible. And with the crowds rooting for the youngsters, Kansa might have lost his nerve."

"It could be, because he ordered his guards to finish off the youngsters; a very indiscreet step considering that the audience included distinguished visitors from the neighbouring kingdoms. Very stupid too, because he was seated close to the wrestling ring and young Krishna, with adrenalin pumping high, had little difficulty in leaping across and finishing him off before the guards could react. Got his just desserts so to speak."

"Mention of dessert reminds me that we are well past our lunch time. The picture of the Lingayat *Thali* on that hoarding of Lingayat Lunch Home looks most appetising. Let us take a break and see if we can do justice to it."

"I also lost track of time but this place seems more than adequate," said JT as *nandighosh* came to a gentle halt. "Let's go."

***

"What is it about a *Paan* that makes a meal feel complete?" asked DK rhetorically, obviously enjoying his after meal betel leaf, *as nandighosh* made its way back onto the highway towards Harihar.

"It is all in your mind DK, although it is supposed to have digestive properties, depending on the ingredients. And after that *thali* of Curd Rice with a *baghar* of red chilies and the accompanying paper thin *papadums* and pickles, you certainly deserve a *Paan*."

"And after killing Kansa, Krishna surely deserved to be the king of Mathura, so why did he not become one? Another of those things about Krishna that I don't understand."

"In fact, if anything, that really showed Krishna's coming of age as an individual," said JT.

"How?"

"The young boy who had left Vrindavan a few weeks back was physically strong but he knew very little of the ways of the world since his exposure had been so limited. However, within a few weeks of being in Mathura, he had learnt such a huge amount. He had understood that politics was his metier but he also realised that he was not yet ready to make any big move. To understand one's limitations is a huge step in anyone's growth."

"Hmm. I am beginning to see."

"Krishna understood that his inexperience in big city and matters of kingdom would sabotage any attempt at taking charge despite the pleadings of many well-wishers, for he had become a hero now. He could see that Kansa's widowed wives, both daughters of the mighty King of Magadh, Jarasandha, still had many sympathisers. Mathura was on the verge of becoming very chaotic. Krishna deduced that a seasoned hand was needed to steady the state," explained JT.

"And he found one in his grandfather, Kansa's father, Ugrasen."

"Yes, Kansa had overthrown him in his greed and kept him imprisoned."

"Oh, so Aurangzeb wasn't the first ruler to depose his father?" DK quipped.

"And certainly, not the last. Power makes people lose their heads often, which makes Krishna's sober handling of the situation, at such a young age, so remarkable and a tribute to his quick learning ability."

"Yes, it is becoming clearer now. So did the situation in Mathura come under control?"

"It did for a while as old King Ugrasen took charge and restored order in Mathura and the entire kingdom. But trouble was round the corner. King Jarasandha, among the most powerful rulers of the time and Kansa's father-in-law, was angry at the turn of events. His son-in-law, who was under his thumb most of the time, had been killed, his two daughters had been widowed and the kingdom of Mathura was no longer his playground."

"I can think of plenty of political parallels with recent global situations from Afghanistan to Iraq," DK interjected.

"Human nature hasn't changed all that much. Jarasandha then decided to march on to Mathura."

"The news must have scared the hell out of Mathura residents."

"It did and it scared King Ugrasen and his cabinet too. Mind you, Krishna had no formal role in Mathura's affairs but given what had transpired till then, his voice was definitely heard and taken seriously by many."

"What could Krishna alone do against a mighty invading force?" DK asked.

"Brains are never to be under-rated in the battle against brawn. King Ugrasen had come to respect his grandson Krishna's brains. Krishna realised that confronting a superior force head-on would be stupidity. He had already used that common sense in his bout with Chanoor, ducking, weaving and staying out of Chanoor's reach till the time was ripe. He advised the same strategy of a defensive battle," JT explained.

"How does that work when armies are involved?" queried DK.

"First, drawing in of all the home forces, securing important people like the king and the cabinet inside the fortified palace. Sieges or such defensive postures may not have been completely new then and Krishna may have learnt about them from his contemporaries. The use of a scorched earth policy, however, seems to have been a novelty then."

"Scorched earth? What exactly is that?" DK asked.

"Making life difficult for the enemy by ensuring that all essential supplies are scarce to secure. Disrupting or damaging water and food supplies including those for animals, creating roadblocks and so on. Plus of course harassing enemy troops with hit-and-run guerrilla tactics. When the match-up of forces was grossly uneven, there was little point in engaging in frontal battle; Krishna seems to have grasped this lesson very early in life."

"So what happened?"

"When Jarasandha's army reached Mathura, it waited for the Mathura army to come and fight. And waited. And waited. After a few days they realised the ploy and they began entering the city. But here the army faced many issues it was not trained for. Soldiers are trained for fighting in open spaces, not for entering narrow lanes where they might be subjected to unpleasant objects being thrown at them from hidden corners. With no water to drink and supplies being rationed, they found the going tough."

"Aah, I understand. Urban guerilla tactics seem to be hard to confront even now," said DK.

"Yes, it is not easy even now with modern weapons. It would have been very tough in those days."

"One question though. How did the Mathurawasis and those staying in the palace manage their food and water needs?"

"That is where real smartness came in. Under Krishna's leadership, plenty of food had been stored by the residents in advance, from the time they got wind of an impending attack. They even got and stored supplies from nearby villages and kingdoms. As for water, there were freshwater wells within the palace compound, the whole rear side of the palace and the city opened onto Yamuna River. Familiarity with paths and small lanes meant that the residents never ran short of essentials."

"What a smart strategy! Then what happened?"

"Jarasandha huffed and puffed — I mean his army of course. For 27 days they tried repeatedly to make inroads against the new strategy they had never anticipated, before finally giving up. They returned to Magadh crestfallen, swearing revenge against Mathura in general and Krishna in particular, for by now it was known that Krishna had been the architect of the strategy."

"Understandable. But King Ugrasen must have been elated!"

"Yes, he was. He had never been very fond of his *samdhi* anyway, always suspected his hand in Kansa's usurping power and now the enmity was out in the open."

"And what about Krishna?" DK wanted to know.

"Krishna had become a sensation not just in Mathura but in public imagination everywhere. And from that point on, irrespective of whether he held any official position or not, the entire Bharatvarsh recognised him as a political powerhouse with an unparalleled and unprecedented grasp of strategy."

"Tell me, I have seen both terms, Bharatvarsh and Aryavarta used to describe our ancient land. Which one is more accurate?"

"Both are often used interchangeably, but I prefer to use Bharatvarsh. King Bharat was an ancestor of the Kuru dynasty so it certainly predates the times we are talking about. While many writers have used the term to denote lands between Himalayas and Vindhyas, I prefer to use the term to broadly denote the entire landmass today called the subcontinent and stretching a bit more in fact. The finer distinctions are not really germane to our discussion."

"Okay, thanks. So much has become clearer now, but the roads are becoming dimmer. We have been travelling in the dark for a while and there don't seem to be any lights on this stretch. Let us call it a day at the first decent halt which comes along."

"Here it is, Harihar Petrol Pump. What better place for a night halt than at a place with Hari, associated with it!"

❑❑❑

CHAPTER 4

Education

"I had an interesting experience this morning," said DK as they hit the road towards Tumkur on the fourth morning. *Nandighosh* was purring along nicely and smelt nice too, after the thorough cleaning it had received. DK looked troubled and the shrewd eyes next to him missed nothing.

"All well in USA I hope?" queried JT, looking at DK sideways from the driver's seat.

"Actually yes, but I was a bit restless after the evening video call to USA. Although Neeta assured me there was nothing to worry about, that Meera was being monitored regularly, I could not sleep easily. So, I stepped out and ran into the petrol pump owner Mr. Murthy. I had a wonderful chat with him."

"What about?"

"Did you know that there are a lot of places around here with Mahabharat association?"

"Which ones are you talking about?"

"Near the village of Makali" continued DK, "there is this tiny place called Bheemeshwara. There is a Shiva temple there from the Vijayanagara period and the lingam there is believed to have been consecrated by Bheem himself. The place was originally on river Arkavathy which has gone dry now. Near the riverbed is a giant depression called Bheemanna Hejje or Bheem's footprint. Amazing." DK's voice was full of awe.

"Yes, they did get around," said JT as he deftly negotiated yet another turn. The terrain was undulating, beautiful green rice fields could be seen in the distance but there was some climb too and the going was a little slow.

"But not Krishna, not at least till his Mathura heroics with Kansa and then foiling of Jarasandha's attempts."

"Yes, he may not have travelled, but his fame did. By this time he was known all over Bharatvarsh."

"But tell me, Jarasandha was described as the most powerful King in Bharatvarsh. I read that he was defeated by Krishna 18 times. How was Jarasandha the most powerful then?"

"Jarasandha was obsessed with Krishna after Kansa's death. He did make multiple attempts spread over years at different places but was unsuccessful."

"So Krishna did defeat him!" DK exclaimed.

"Thwarted his designs would be more accurate. In the first attack on Mathura though, it was a brilliant defensive strategy devised by Krishna against a superior army, as I mentioned yesterday."

"What did Jarasandha do next?"

"Jarasandha withdrew temporarily like any astute army general, vowing to return with a bigger force. He also made no secret of his belief that it was Krishna who was mainly responsible for the way things had turned out and singled him out for his direst threats."

"Hmm. And what did Mathurawasis think about that?"

"Common folk were probably high on adrenalin from having thwarted Jarasandha's attack and there were many who by then sincerely believed in Krishna's divinity. They were really not worried."

"Many but not all?"

"The problem is obvious. Some people surely asked themselves that if Krishna was indeed divine, why did he not finish off Jarasandha himself? The moment divinity is brought in, all questioning stops. There were many, including noblemen, who thought that Mathura may have been lucky once and there was not much point in tempting fate. They, of course, conveyed their apprehensions to the king."

"Interesting. Things are never in clear black and white as most narratives are. What did the king think though?"

"King Ugrasen was wise and having personally experienced Jarasandha's wrath, was wary as well. He was Krishna's grandfather, concerned about Krishna's life as also about his future. He came up with a unique solution."

"What was that?" DK was genuinely intrigued.

"He decided to send Krishna to Rishi Sandipani's *ashram* at Avantika, near present day Ujjain, for education."

"But surely there would be little security in an exposed place like an *ashram!*"

"That was the beauty of the plan. By accepted convention of the day, teachers' *ashrams* were sanctified areas which even kings dared not invade or harm. Even Jarasandha would not have been willing to court the anger of the entire Bharatvarsh by flouting that convention."

"Now I get it. Besides Krishna and Balaram had had little formal education till then and a grandfather would have wanted to remedy that."

"Yes, they were essentially strong cowherds till that point, with Krishna clearly demonstrating his intelligence and instinctive strategic acumen. Krishna's potential must have been obvious to the king and he correctly recognised the need for some formal education to round it off better. No amount of talent alone is enough without a certain amount of nurturing. Also remember, Rishi Sandipani's *ashram* was a much sought after place those days, and while most students were from royal and noble families, there were a few children of common citizens too. Obviously Krishna and Balaram could not have got 'admission' there without some royal sponsorship."

DK nodded in understanding. "The absence of Krishna and Balaram from Mathura, which Jarasandha's spies were sure to report, would dilute his motivation to attack Mathura again. Once executed, the plan must have simultaneously reassured the nervous noblemen and citizens of Mathura! The pieces are all falling into place now."

"Yes but apart from its strategic importance from the perspective of Mathura, this phase of life was to be crucial for Krishna too."

"How? I must confess I have read only cursory references to it."

"Actually quite a few interesting things happened in this phase that make it easier to understand and connect the dots in episodes which happened later in Krishna's life."

"What important things?" DK was curious.

"First, Krishna gained enormous knowledge of scriptures and all the disciplines in vogue at that time very fast. He was clearly a high IQ student and absorbed knowledge like a sponge."

"I did wonder about that. When one comes across some profound statements later on, in Krishna's interactions with Arjun or Karna or Bhishma Pitamah, it can be quite puzzling if one is unaware of his formal education."

"Yes," agreed JT. "Once we know that there was formal learning from acknowledged masters which could have been the basis on which Krishna developed his own concepts, it makes it so much easier to understand subsequent developments."

"I believe the *ashram* near Ujjain is a very serene place even today. Must have been a perfect place to understand complex subjects then."

"Of course. And many others who played minor or major parts in Krishna's life later were a part of this phase: Sudama, Princes Vinda and Anuvinda, Prince Rukmi. His sister, Princess Rukmini too, who very likely visited the *ashram* a few times. Later Krishna went on to marry Rukmini in a rather dramatic fashion."

"Yes, and I had been puzzled about references to her having fallen in love with him, sending an SOS, all without any personal encounters at all? I am glad that this has been cleared up."

"Krishna also obtained his Sudarshan Chakra and the famous conch Panchajanya during this period."

"I thought he had received the Sudarshan Chakra from Surya Devata?" asked DK. "After the Khandavprasth incident."

"Yes there is that version too, better known probably. But there are other versions which say he got it from Parshuram. Parshuram Rishi also had his *ashram* for students nearby, some versions claim he also taught at Sandipani Rishi's *ashram* which does not seem improbable, considering that Parshuram Rishi's birthplace Jalapav is not too far away from Ujjain. Visiting faculty sort of. Parshuram could well have gifted a special weapon to a special student."

"And what about the conch or *shankh* Panchajanya?"

"It really doesn't have too much to do with our discussion about Krishna's divinity, so I will just summarise the happenings briefly."

"We can skip it if you wish."

"No, there are a few aspects in that part of Krishna's life story which will help in understanding what is to follow. After their education, Krishna and Balaram enquired from Sandipani Rishi about what he would like as *Guru Dakshina*, as was the norm those days. It transpired that long ago *gurudev's* son had been kidnapped by a sea dwelling 'demon' named *shankhasur* and the Rishi and his wife pined for his return. Some versions say the boy was kept imprisoned in the *shankh* Panchajanya. Krishna and Balaram killed the demon after many adventures, rescued the boy and returned with lots of wealth and Panchajanya *shankh*."

"Okay. Coming back to the Sudarshan Chakra, I am intrigued by such an advanced weapon, a circular disc with supposedly very sharp serrations being around at that time."

"We should not be, whether we look at it through an archaeological lens or through our ancient literature."

"Why?"

"See, advanced metal work can be seen even in the 3-4000 year old weapons which have been recovered from archaeological sites in different parts of India."

"I remember reading something like that."

"And talking of our ancient literature and epics, we need to understand that Time itself has been divided in our scriptures into four *Yugas*. Krita or Sat Yuga, Treta Yuga, Dwapar Yuga and Kali Yuga. The important thing to remember is that in many respects the rules of the game itself change from one *Yuga* to another."

"I did not understand."

"Look at it this way. In Krita or Sat Yuga there was no *paap* so there really was not much difference between *Swarglok* and *Prithvi*. It could have been possible for people, perhaps selected people, scholars or *rishi-munis*, to travel from one to the other."

"That needs some thought."

"While at it, do also think about Pole Reversal or search it on Google. It has happened many times in the earth's past and would have surely messed up life on earth and all the everyday laws of physics which we take for granted."

"What are you trying to suggest?"

"Nothing really, except that when we run into something from another *Yuga* which does not fit in with our knowledge of materials and physical properties today, instead of saying 'impossible', we should perhaps say 'that was in another

Yuga, may be things happened like that then, we can't know for sure'."

"Hmm, point noted. So we have Krishna now returning to Mathura with a lot of formal knowledge, weapons and considerable wealth."

"Yes, don't forget Balaram. The two of them were together right through, though it may not be incorrect to say that it was Krishna who developed more, learnt more."

"Lots of food for thought today, time for some food for the body. I am famished and this fancy looking Tumkur Hut seems to be just the place. Their *Devanagere Bene Dosa* seems to be quite famous, let us give it a shot."

***

"This part of India is so beautiful!" remarked DK as *nandighosh* resumed its journey along the winding roads. The road was narrow, but JT maneuvered the large vehicle easily.

"It is."

"And there are many temples too boasting of some connections with Mahabharat or Ramayan."

"Yes, but veracity of all the claims is hard to establish. Even so we ought to be grateful to them for preserving our connections with the epics, however stretched or exaggerated some versions may seem at times."

"I believe there are hundreds of so-called 'original' versions of Ramayan and Mahabharat preserved in different temples of India."

"Very true. It took scholars at Bhandarkar Oriental Research Institute in Pune decades to sift through hundreds of so called 'original' volumes of Mahabharat to figure out which version might be closest to what Ved Vyas might have written."

"Must have been tough. I have been thinking about what you said about Krishna and Balaram returning with lots of wealth and I am puzzled."

"Why?"

"How did they bring all the wealth to Mathura?"

"Chariot-loads of them. The chariots were also earned by them as part of their victories. In fact, for their journey from Sandipani Rishi's *ashram* to Mathura, the king of Avanti, in whose territory the *ashram* was located, also gave a few chariots to them. His sons, Vinda and Anuvinda, were classmates of Krishna and Balaram at the *ashram*."

"Then surely all the Mathurawasis knew of their wealth, in which case why was Krishna accused of the theft of a jewel, something which has remained as a bit of a blot on his name?" DK wondered.

JT sighed. "Like many things, it is a bit more complicated than that and we need to understand the full context of the Syamantaka jewel story before reaching any conclusion."

"I am all ears."

"The Syamantaka story is spread over Krishna's Mathura and Dwarka periods, though strictly speaking, the location doesn't matter too much while trying to understand what might have happened. Keep that at the back of your mind, but first understand the context of what Mathura was like when Krishna and Balaram returned."

"Had it changed from the time they left it?"

"Very much so. It had gone to seed. The damage done by Jarasandha's troops had not been repaired. Every war or battle costs money, even defensive ones; the economy of the town had been severely damaged and the treasury of King Ugrasen was empty."

"But surely there were wealthy merchants in the town willing to help out the king!"

"Yes and No. Yes, there were wealthy merchants in the city and no, they were not ready to share their wealth with the king."

"But what about the subjects?"

"The subjects were divided. There were better off Yadav leaders like Satrajit who had their own camps and followers, while the *aam janta* was struggling to make two ends meet."

"Why does that sound familiar? That seems to be a very contemporary story of most countries!"

"It has been so for most of history."

"Okay so Krishna and Balaram returned to what seems like a rundown Mathura with a weak, enfeebled king, an empty treasury and a divided populace. Surely they must have welcomed Krishna with open arms!"

"The king and the *aam janta* did, not so the Yadav nobility. They were afraid he might disrupt their rather comfortable existence, given that Krishna's presence in Mathura would be a red flag to Jarasandha."

"So what did they do?" DK asked.

"Although Krishna had no formal position, his past deeds had made his voice an important one. During his education and subsequent adventures, Krishna had learnt the importance of wealth and argued in favour of strengthening the state treasury."

"That could not have please the well-to-do."

"It did not, and some thought Krishna had become too fond of money. But Krishna was interested in wealth, not so much for himself, as for the good it could do to the people. He suggested raising taxes on the more affluent among the people which obviously annoyed an influential section of the population. Who likes paying taxes?"

"Now I am beginning to see the connection with the allegations against Krishna regarding the Syamantaka jewel. I have a rough idea but what exactly was the jewel?" DK asked pointedly.

JT laughed. "Okay, here goes. And Surya Devata has a role in it so it is a good story to remember as we see the sun setting to our west. The story goes that Satrajit, a Yadav nobleman, was a Surya *bhakt* and pleased with his devotion, Surya Devata gifted him the Syamantaka jewel which could give eight ounces or about a quarter of a kilo of gold every day."

"How is that possible?"

"Remember what we talked earlier of different *Yugas*, different rules? So let us go with the flow please, our focus has to be on Krishna and his actions."

"Alright, carry on."

"The story continues that Krishna suggested to Satrajit that such a source of wealth, and the wealth it produced, should be used for the larger good so why not give it to the King Ugrasen? You could also interpret it as Krishna saying that a mint should not be in private hands and that it must always be under the control of the lawful rulers."

"Yes, some of the recent experiences with cryptocurrencies underline the importance of that point of view. So what was Satrajit's response?"

"Satrajit declined. A little later the jewel went missing. Satrajit had given it to his brother who had gone missing and evidently the jewel had been stolen from him. Satrajit suspected Krishna of having stolen the jewel."

"Smells like politics to me."

"Yes, and the slur lasted quite a while. Ultimately, Krishna managed to track down the jewel in the jungles after much strife, recovered it and gave it back to Satrajit. A contrite Satrajit then gave his daughter Satyabhama in marriage to

Krishna. Mind you, by this time the move to Dwarka had already taken place, and Krishna had married Rukmini. So, this story happened over a fair period of time. I have just given you a quick summary because other than clearing Krishna of a false charge, there is not much of long term value in the episode."

"Okay, so Krishna restored stolen property. But he did not have any claim to it anyway," argued DK.

"But he did, although that happened a while later. By this time the move to Dwarka had taken place and Krishna had married both Rukmini and Satyabhama. When he was away from Dwarka, one of the other Yadavas, Shatadhvana, killed Satrajit and stole the jewel. Angry Satyabhama reached out to Krishna who returned to Dwarka to look for his father-in-law's killer. Fearing the worst, Shatadhvana fled into the forest but before that gave the gem to Akrur for safekeeping. Krishna eventually killed Shatadhvana but obviously there was no gem to recover this time."

"That must have been tough."

"This time even Balaram suspected that Krishna might have stolen it. Meanwhile, Akrur did many *pujas* and *yagnas* which led Krishna to suspect him, so he called him out. Akrur finally accepted that the gem was given to him for safekeeping whereupon Satyabhama argued that the gem belonged to her father, so it was now rightfully hers or effectively Krishna's. But Krishna declined, saying it had come into Akrur's possession for safekeeping, so it should remain with him."

"That does not sound right. Stolen property after all."

"That is right and that was the final ruling by the king and the court anyway. Thus, by a convoluted route, as Satyabhama's husband, Krishna did become the legitimate possessor of that unique gem."

DK was enchanted with the story. "Yes, this incident does prove that Krishna had no particular attachment to wealth. So true and such a good note to end our day's journey on," he added. "Krishna could conquer so many things but I need to conquer my curiosity about what comes next. For the moment, as it becomes dark here and a new day begins in the US, worries about what is happening in the US with Meera return."

"All will be well, do not worry."

"I hope so too. Let us break for the night here, *Appams* and Vegetable Stew as shown on the hoarding at this Kannada Food House looks tempting!"

❑❑❑

CHAPTER 5

Dwarka

"Did Krishna have a moustache?" DK asked impatiently as they started off the next day. JT had taken the wheels of *nandighosh* as had become the norm.

"I wouldn't know" said JT. "Why do you ask?"

"I had an interesting encounter on my morning walk. I met a gentleman at the roadside coffee stall, we got talking when I commented about Krishna's image on the calendar hanging there. I had never seen a Krishna figure with a moustache before."

"In the absence of photos or videos, people had little choice but to exercise their imagination in depicting characters from our epics they had come to revere and love. In Nashik you can find a brilliant black stone idol of Shri Ram at the Kalaram Mandir. Go eastwards, right up to Bali, Indonesia and even Japan, you will find Shri Ram with Oriental features. In southern India itself you may find figures of Bheem often resembling some WWF dark skinned wrestler! In the larger context, the message is more important than the packaging."

"I understand. This gentleman got very excited when I said we may be going to Dharmapuri today," said DK.

"Why? The thought of negotiating traffic close to Bengaluru does not sound very appealing to me."

"It is not about the traffic, but the wonderful Chennakesava Temple in Dharmapuri. It has amazing murals depicting scenes from Ramayan and Mahabharat on its ceilings.

Extraordinary, the lengths to which our ancients went to preserve our heritage," DK shook his head.

"Yes, and one day you must see Mathura and Dwarka to get the complete feel," remarked JT.

"Now that you have brought up Dwarka, I have been meaning to ask you. How did that shift happen?"

"It is all related to Jarasandha's obsession with Krishna and trying to destroy him as a payback for what had happened to his son-in-law Kansa."

"One would have thought that once Krishna and Balaram left Mathura for Rishi Sandipani's *ashram*, Jarasandha would have cooled down!" exclaimed DK.

"No, that did not happen. In fact as soon as they returned, educated and wealthy after having rescued Sandipani Rishi's son and killing the demon Shankhasur, Jarasandha started plotting an attack on Mathura."

"Hmm. So how did Krishna fight him this time?"

"Krishna did not fight him this time either, but outwitted him instead. Krishna and Balaram left Mathura and on the advice of sages, some accounts say Parshuram, took refuge in the Gomanta mountain. Jarasandha came to know of their hideout and followed with a huge army."

"But surely if Krishna had been divine or an *avataar*, he could have killed Jarasandha, who was no less evil than say Kansa or later Duryodhan."

"Exactly the reason why Krishna's gradual evolution into an extraordinary person seems far more credible than merely ascribing divinity to him and thereby skipping any analysis. And there is no doubt that Jarasandha was evil. He had planned a supreme *yagna* once he had 100 kings in captivity and he could sacrifice them all."

"So Krishna and Balaram escaped again?"

"Yes, and it is these escapades which earned Krishna the name *Ranchoddas*."

"Isn't running away from battle a sign of cowardice?" DK persisted.

"Yes and No. If someone shows his back to the enemy and runs away from a battlefield out of fear of losing his life, that is cowardice; but if someone wants to bide his time, avoids frontal confrontation till the time is ripe, it just shows strategic acumen and intelligence. That is what Krishna showed again by escaping to Gomanta mountain."

"And what was the outcome this time?" DK posited.

"Same result. Thanks to the help of some locals and tribals, brilliant use of their position on a higher altitude, rolling of boulders and some smart use of fire, Krishna and Balaram were able to force Jarasandha's army to flee. In the process, Krishna-Balaram also found some hidden treasure on the mountain and returned to Mathura very wealthy."

"Surely Jarasandha had been adequately chastened by now. So where was the need for Krishna to get hyper about Jarasandha anymore?"

"It shows both his growing maturity and understanding of human nature. Krishna knew that Jarasandha was not the type to lie low for long. Therefore, he must have examined many contingency Plan Bs and Cs, while life in Mathura went on smoothly, even if only on the surface."

"Oh yes! I had forgotten about Krishna's rival Satrajit."

"Yes, Krishna's was an important voice in Mathura and he had devoted followers like his cousin Uddhav. But there were rivals for influence among Yadavs too. Satrajit was the foremost, though Krishna was successful in wooing away one of his main supporters, Satyaki."

"That name rings a loud bell. Wasn't he one of the stalwarts of the Mahabharat war?"

"Yes, by many accounts next only to Arjun as a master archer. Fought valiantly and was among the seven men who were said to have survived the war from Pandava's side."

"So did they decide one day to move away from Mathura to far off Dwarka, just like that?" DK's voice reflected his disbelief.

"No, no, it certainly did not happen suddenly. The whole thing evolved over a period of time. A few years in fact."

"How did that happen?"

"One day Krishna and Balaram decided to visit Rishi Sandipani's *ashram*."

"Visiting one's Alma Mater does not seem to be so new."

"Not at all, it used to happen throughout history and I am sure they enjoyed visiting the spots where Sudama must have sung some beautiful songs for them while Krishna had played the flute. Sudama was indeed a very good singer."

"Reminds me of my college days."

"But this time around two girls were also studying in Sandipani *ashram*."

"Oh! I did not know there was co-education in India at that time!"

"Where do you think the *vidushis* that we read about in ancient literature studied? Yes, it was probably not very common but education for women was certainly not barred in ancient India."

"Okay... there were two girls on campus now. What happened next?"

"One of them was Revati, only child of King Kakumadi, who ruled a small kingdom Kushasthali, on the west coast of India. Kushasthali had been annexed by a hostile neighbour, Punyajan. Also, King Kakumadi was, to put it delicately, struggling with keeping his mental faculties intact. Balaram fell hard for Revati and she fell in love with him too."

"Oh, that is an unexpected twist. Campus romance in ancient India! So far it has always been about Krishna though."

"When Krishna and Balaram returned to Mathura, they persuaded King Ugrasen to send a small force of about a thousand under Balaram and Uddhav to the west coast of India to help out Revati. Punyajan was defeated, Balaram married Revati and, given the king's diminished capacity, became the de facto ruler of Kushasthali."

"Very interesting. All new to me."

"Krishna had confided in Balaram and Uddhav about needing a possible contingency plan as an insurance against Jarasandha's threats. Therefore, Balaram and Uddhav took the opportunity to do some reconnaissance and soon struck pay dirt."

"They found Dwarka?" DK asked.

"Of course not. What they did find was a wonderful piece of land, just off the coast, surrounded by sea, with very good defense possibilities. When they returned to Mathura, they shared their findings with Krishna."

"Aah, now I can see the divine miracle coming as Dwarka was built overnight by Krishna."

"No such thing, we Indians are given to too much hyperbole," sighed JT. "Once the place was described to him, Krishna immediately recognised the potential of the place as a defensive stronghold. But nothing happens overnight, not now, not then."

"What did Krishna do?"

"He did what any highly intelligent person would do. He planned quietly, without taking too many people in confidence. The first thing was to seek out a good architect and there were two very big names around at that time, Maya and Vishwakarma."

"But wasn't Maya the architect of the *rakshasas*?" DK was puzzled.

"It is human nature to stigmatise the 'other' and has been so for thousands of years. Colour of skin, features, method of dressing, anything different has been enough to stigmatise the 'other' in human history. The European explorers, British, Dutch, Portuguese were called 'barbarians' by the Japanese and Chinese in the 16th and 17th century and they in turn spoke about the Easterners with similar pejorative descriptions, slanty-eyed, chinkies and so on. Let us just say Maya was different."

"Right JT, who did Krishna choose?"

"Krishna went to see Vishwakarma. His township was a little away from Mathura, on the way to Kushasthali, which suited Krishna fine, for the purpose of his visit could remain secret."

"And what was Krishna's brief to Vishwakarma?"

"It might sound audacious if we were not too familiar with the narrative already. Krishna told him he wanted to build a capital city for a new kingdom, for he had decided by now that an entirely new kingdom was necessary."

"Breath-taking audacity for sure. But what was the reason?"

"Look at the larger picture. Krishna was already the talk of Bharatvarsh because of his killing of Kansa and outsmarting of Jarasandha, but he was still not nobility really. Maybe his encounters with the beautiful princess Rukmini while at Sandipani *ashram* had also triggered the urge to become a part of royalty, so to speak, in order to bring some parity to his eligibility; and yet, Krishna did not want to get into overthrowing or killing any king for the sake of a kingdom. So he set about creating a new one."

"What a marvellous example to set! I had never thought of this aspect truly. So Krishna briefed Vishwakarma to design a capital?"

"A worthy one too with broad roads, gardens, a palace, the works."

"And, many of us thought Chandigarh was the first properly planned city!"

"There were budget constraints, of course. Although Krishna had recovered treasures from his campaigns against *Shankhasur* and in the Gomanta mountain, obviously the wealth available wasn't limitless. Fortunately, Dwarka wasn't meant to be the largest capital even by contemporary standards. In the end the money just about sufficed."

"How long did it take to construct Dwarka?"

"Most accounts place it at around 18 months, which is really sensational, if you consider that; any ordinary residential tower in a big city in India even today takes about that much time."

"In a sense, it was a miracle and people were not wrong in calling it so."

"Yes, it was. But it is not to be taken literally as if Krishna had waved a magic wand and the city appeared out of the blue."

"It was still a blue sky venture though. Talking of blue skies, this Blue Sky Hotel here looks like a great place for us to take our lunch break."

"Yes, I was wondering about that. Talking and driving is hungry work," remarked JT as he eased *nandighosh* into the parking lot outside the hotel.

***

"That lunch was truly magical," said a very satisfied DK as the *nandighosh* resumed its journey.

JT laughed. "Yes it was. Maybe a compensation for having robbed you of the magic in the creation of Dwarka."

"So they moved to Dwarka immediately?" asked DK, serious again

"No, in fact Jarasandha may have got wind of the happenings and he seems to have scaled up his efforts. This time around he got the help of Kalayavana, among the strongest of kings around. The plan was to catch Mathura in a pincer movement. But Krishna got to know of these plans in time and brought forward the move to shift, even before Dwarka was fully ready."

"Oh, it seems espionage is not new either."

"I am afraid not. When Krishna disclosed the plan to the Yadav elders, there was surprisingly little resistance. Most people could see that Mathura was going to seed, and as happens when a place or society starts declining, drinking, gambling were also becoming very noticeable and hard to control. To all the leaders, therefore, the plan to make a fresh start, move to an entirely new place away from the ever present threat of immediate war and destruction seemed very attractive."

"What did King Ugrasen say?"

"He fell in with the plans immediately. Not just him but even Krishna's rivals like Satrajit joined the chorus. We need to understand that while Ugrasen was the formal king, Yadavas were really more like an oligarchy than a monarchy; a group of seniors or other influential leaders were also involved in the decision making."

"Hmmm... how long did the move to Dwarka take?"

"One can find different estimates but it probably took about a month or month and a half. Moving 20-25,000 people would have required considerable management of resources like carts and food and so on."

"Would be a logistical feat even today!" exclaimed DK.

"Yes. Once they settled in, there were lavish feasts and rulers from the entire Bharatvarsh were invited for a formal launch of Dwarka, so to speak. In fact cousins Pandavas were also invited and spent some time with Krishna, Balaram, Uddhav and Satyaki, developing strong and lasting bonds. Kunti, mother of the three elder Pandav brothers, Yudhishthir, Bheem and Arjun, was Vasudev's sister.

"Yes, of course. I now understand the significance of the Dwarka chapter in Krishna's life. It was no miracle but yet another sign of Krishna's growing mastery over tactics and strategy, the way he outmanoeuvred Jarasandha again."

"It was more than that actually. In their desire to ascribe divinity to Krishna, most commentators have ignored the masterly lessons in administration that Krishna gave while working out Dwarka's early administrative set up and rules."

"I don't understand?" said DK.

"See, Krishna had observed Mathura's decay at close quarters and the role liquor and womanising had played in it. There must have been the temptation to ban some of these in the beginning itself in Dwarka, for such things are easier done at the start. And yet, Krishna did nothing of the sort. He regulated the activities by prescribing timings, taxed them substantially, including courtesans, and offered them a degree of legitimacy and state protection. Considering that Krishna must have been only in his mid-20s at that time, this represents an astounding level of maturity."

"I am getting the sense but explain a bit more please."

"Some so called 'vices' seem natural to men and no one in history has been able to banish them completely. In fact many people believe it was the 'prohibition' which led to the creation of the underworld in USA and elsewhere. Such well-meaning regulations often seem to lead to the sprouting of other evils in society, possibly much more dangerous. Krishna seems to have grasped this very early on and instead of a moralistic position, he took a very positive and pragmatic one," explained JT.

"So true, now that I think of it. Maybe most commentators felt that highlighting this aspect of Krishna's life would run counter to their own puritanical beliefs and avoided mention of it altogether?"

"Very likely but details of the early administration in Dwarka are worthy of study on their own merits. Vishnu Parv in Harivansh Purana and a few other sources give detailed descriptions of how commerce was encouraged by selling shops at cost price and so many other measures which must have been revolutionary at the time."

"And it must have added extra aura to Krishna's growing reputation as an 'incarnate' among the common people. You are really opening my eyes to an aspect of Krishna's life I had never paid much attention to."

"You aren't the only one. Most of us never think about Krishna as an administrator," JT remarked with a smile.

"What happened next?"

"For the moment, there was a lull on the political side. However, momentous incidents took place in Krishna's life in the next few years. For starters, it was Rukmini episode which most people are familiar with."

"The much talked of *swayamvar*?"

"Yes, it was. King Bhishmak of Kundinpur, Rukmini's father, was perhaps not aware of the political plotting by Jarasandha and Rukmi, brother of Rukmini, to get her married off to Shishupal. But Rukmini was made of sterner stuff; she sent her envoys, Shwetketu and Shaivya, to Krishna in Dwarka with an SOS for a rescue."

"So those accounts are true after all," said DK, pleased that he had got that right.

"The SOS part seems to be true but not the breathless overnight rescue that some versions talk about. Krishna had time to organise the rescue party including Balaram, Uddhav, Satyaki and a few soldiers. When Krishna abducted Rukmini from the temple early morning as most versions say, this team ran interference and prevented Rukmi's escort team from stopping Krishna's chariot as it raced towards Dwarka."

"Yet again Jarasandha's nose was rubbed in the dirt!"

"With Shishupal for company this time around. But Rukmi was not to be so easily discouraged. He chased Krishna's chariot and caught up with them after a while. He issued wild threats but Krishna managed to subdue him without much difficulty. In fact Krishna could have killed him too but Rukmini pleaded for the life of her elder brother so Krishna relented and let him go."

"So finally Krishna was able to bring his bride home."

"Yes, truly. After years of struggle, being branded *Ranchoddas*, being chased all over the country, in fact being forced to build a new capital city for a newly established kingdom, Krishna had finally come home."

"Did Krishna finally get the time off for rest and recreation that he deserved so much?" asked DK.

"Not really, there was not to be too much Rest and Recreation in his life. But let us talk about it tomorrow, for we certainly deserve a bit of R and R after our long tiring day."

"Yes and this Dharmapuri Petrol Pump looks inviting enough. I am sure we can tank up and stay here for the night."

❑❑❑

CHAPTER 6

Grandmaster in the Making

"Change of plans," announced DK as they climbed into *nandighosh* next day.

"Why, what happened?" asked JT, adjusting his seat belt.

"Women!" said DK with mock resignation. "When Neeta found out that we were in Dharmapuri, she did a quick search and found that we were close to Coimbatore. You can guess what comes next. She suggested that we take a small detour and buy some silk saris from Coimbatore. Many occasions for gifting are coming up after the grandchild arrives and she wants to be armed for them."

"Ha ha ha" laughed JT. "It will probably cost us a day or two extra but then time hardly matters to us, right?"

"True, and I have been married long enough to know that Neeta's suggestions like these are commands for all practical purposes, to be disobeyed at one's peril."

"Some things never change," said JT.

"Why, was Krishna also being ordered around by Rukmini?" asked DK, eager to pick up yesterday's conversation thread.

"Ha ha...that I would never know or speculate about. But it is a fact that Krishna's attention after marriage was increasingly drawn to the world outside. In fact, given his increasing reputation as a problem solver across Bharatvarsh, it could not have been otherwise."

"Who wanted his help now?" wondered DK.

“It was his great-grandfather Aaryak, maternal grandfather of Vasudev and advisor to Naagraj Vasuki, who sent Krishna a message asking him to visit.”

“Oh. I thought it was to be about Draupadi. Krishna was in his mid-20s, so time for Mahabharat to enter his life or maybe time for him to enter the Mahabharat story.”

“Yes. But first you must understand the geo-political chessboard that was Bharatvarsh then, before you can grasp Krishna’s role in it at different stages.”

“Yes, from what we have seen till the move to Dwarka, everything seems to point towards an extraordinarily gifted individual, improving himself constantly and finding solutions to challenging situations. So far at least we seem to have found an answer to everything without having to fall back on the one-answer-for-all-questions, Krishna’s supposed divinity.”

“True, but his growth as an individual was not yet complete and the next stage was about to begin,” explained JT.

“And where did the next stage begin?”

“In Hastinapur, where else? Krishna decided that on his way to meet his great-grandfather, he would visit his cousins, the Pandav brothers, in Hastinapur. Some versions have it that he was near Hastinapur with his entourage when the Lakshagrah episode took place.”

“I am generally aware that Duryodhan and Shakuni burnt down a palace made of inflammable materials like lac where Pandavas were supposed to be staying. But refresh it for me a bit please.”

“Sure. Duryodhan was unhappy with the naming of Yudhishthir as the Yuvraj. It was not really surprising considering the full circumstances.”

“What full circumstances?” DK was curious.

"See, the Pandavas were born in the Satsringa forest where Pandu Maharaj had retired after being cursed by a *rishi*, something you surely know, so I will not repeat it. Being forest dwellers did not mean that they were uneducated. Pandu Maharaj himself, among the most illustrious rulers and warriors of the Kuru dynasty, had arranged for the best of *rishis* to teach them. And knowing that someday Yudhishthir, the eldest and the most intelligent of them, might need more than what ordinary *rishis* might be able to teach, Pandu Maharaj personally taught him ethics and practical matters that a ruler ought to know."

"I did not know that," said DK.

"When Kuntidevi brought Pandavas to Hastinapur, post-Pandu Maharaj's death, they were not really raw products. Yudhishthir must have been around 15, Arjun was 13 possibly, already a good archer, thanks to his first teacher in the *ashram*, Suketu."

"I thought Dronacharya was their first teacher."

"Many think so. But no, he wasn't. Kauravas, in contrast, were raw and unruly."

"That must have hurt Duryodhan."

"Put yourself in his shoes. Till yesterday he thought of himself as 'Yuvraj', and suddenly there was this brighter, elder claimant around, quickly winning the favour of the citizenry as well as the court elders with his manners and graceful behaviour. Not just that, till yesterday Duryodhan was the tough guy around town, now there was Bheem who was clearly much stronger."

"I can sense the heartburn across thousands of years!"

"Fact is, normal people don't let such situations force them into crime, unless there is an existing pathological, villainous streak, which Duryodhan had. Throughout the education imparted by Guru Dronacharya, it was evident that the Pandavas were far more gifted than others. It was obvious to Duryodhan that while Bheem and Arjun were with him, Yudhishthir was unbeatable and that he could lose the crown, which from childhood had seemed within his grasp. Out of sight is often out of mind and he had been conditioned, by his surroundings, maybe his parents and everyone else around him, that one day he would be the king. A reality check like the one he got would have jolted far more gifted and wiser boys than him."

"Hence the pathological hatred," DK nodded in understanding. "Then what happened?"

"He had a nasty mentor in his *mama* Shakuni too. Duryodhan first made an attempt to poison Bheem at Pramankoti on the banks of Ganga early on, which failed. And later on, after the completion of their education, dreamt up the plot to have all the Pandavas and their mother burnt in a lac palace."

"Didn't Vidur warn Yudhishthir in advance, which helped them escape through a tunnel?"

"That much is common to practically all versions, so we may accept it at face value. Further, there are accounts that when Krishna, on his way to meet his great-grandfather Aaryak, went to Hastinapur to check out what had happened to his cousins, Vidur confided in him that they had escaped."

"Why did he do that?"

"Given that Krishna was Pandava's cousin and well-wisher and a growing stalwart of Bharatvarsh, he was the perfect choice for Vidur to confide in, if he was to confide in anyone at all."

"That makes sense. The information must have brought a lot of relief to Krishna."

"It surely did, but it also made him aware that there were other games being played on the giant political chessboard which was Bharatvarsh of the time."

"Hmm, yes, so far he had been preoccupied with fending off Jarasandha's threats," said DK.

"Right, and now he became aware of the finer details of the other important match-up, that between Kaurava and Pandava. Being around in Hastinapur, seeing its importance, for it was a much bigger place than either Mathura or Dwarka, must have made Krishna so much more aware of the larger world outside his small world till then. His sensitive political antenna surely picked up some strong, new vibes."

"Kaurava-Pandava rivalry, yes, but what else?"

"In fact there was another game within a game going on, the Dronacharya versus Drupad rivalry," pointed out JT.

"Oh yes!"

"By this time, the story of Drona and Drupad had also spread across much of Bharatvarsh and Krishna may have heard of it in Dwarka itself. Obviously he would have learnt many more details in Hastinapur."

"If I recall correctly, Drupad had snubbed his childhood friend Dronacharya when the latter had come to his court asking him to keep his promise of sharing his kingdom. When Drupad refused, Dronacharya was consumed with rage and he took his revenge when after the education of Kauravas and Pandavas was complete, he asked for Drupad to be brought captive before him as *Guru Dakshina*."

"Yes, and Arjun fulfilled that task. Dronacharya freed Drupad after taking half his kingdom, in turn stoking the desire for revenge in Drupad."

"How naive of Dronacharya to think that Drupad would forget and forgive such humiliation," said DK.

"He did not, but contrary to popular perception, it seems doubtful if he prayed for a son-in-law to bring Dronacharya to book."

"Hmm...but that is the version I read, culminating in Arjun marrying Draupadi."

"Sounds illogical. Any king in such a situation would either plot a revenge himself, possibly with some strong friend or ally or pray for a son capable enough to do it. A son-in-law would at best be Plan C."

"That makes sense. Was Drupad's son, Dhrishtadyumn, capable enough?" asked DK.

"Both Shikhandi, Drupad's daughter-turned son and Dhrishtadyumn were very capable military generals and warriors. You surely know about that Amba-Bhishma saga, resulting in Amba being reborn as Shikhandi, so I will not repeat it. Shikhandi had in fact thrashed the Kauravas when they made the first attempt to capture Drupad as *Guru Dakshina* for Dronacharya and caught them all. It was only Yudhishthir's kind-hearted intervention which led to Arjun and Bheem releasing the Kauravas, after they had defeated the army led by Shikhandi first and then captured Drupad."

"Why did Yudhishthir do that? The entire Mahabharat could have been avoided then and there!"

"Maybe, maybe not. The point I am making is that while both sons of Drupad were capable in their own way, they were not in the same league as either Arjun or his Guru, Dronacharya."

"That must have put Drupad in a quandary."

"Put yourself in Drupad's shoes. Realising that his sons were good but not good enough, who could he turn to in the entire Bharatvarsh?"

"How would I know? Wait a minute...Krishna! He had already shown exceptional ability in outwitting Jarasandha without really engaging in battle."

"Exactly. To that extent, logic would tend to support the versions, or speculation if you wish, which suggest that Drupad approached Krishna with a marriage proposal for Draupadi with a clear string attached that Dronacharya would need to be brought to book."

"And how did Krishna respond?" asked DK, fascinated by this unexpected twist.

"Krishna must have figured out in Hastinapur that Kauravas were pure evil. From there on, it was easy for him to deduce that as long as they had the backing of Bhishma, Dronacharya and Karna, who was also being talked of as an A-lister in *Dhanurvidya*, Kauravas were practically unbeatable. Unless there was another A-lister in *Dhanurvidya* in the opposing camp. Someone like Arjun."

"Sounds cold logic when you put it that way."

"So when Drupad put forward the marriage to Draupadi proposal, Krishna demurred. He could not really reveal that Pandavas might be alive so he could well have floated the idea of a *swayamvar* with a tough archery contest as the bait to get the right man. Or maybe Drupad himself came to the same conclusion once Krishna had demurred. In strategic terms, it was clear that he needed a top archer, *dhanurdhar* really, proficient in *Astra* and *Shastra vidya,* in his corner and a *swayamvar* which might attract the best in Bharatvarsh might be just the solution to his dilemma. Drupad may not even have thought of Arjun at this point, for the Pandavas were thought to be dead. In any case, Arjun's standing with Drupad till then was mainly as Dronacharya's pet student who had recently whipped him."

"The whole thing is now beginning to make sense."

"Such an event requires planning of course. In due course, the contraption with the rotating fish at a height was designed and custom-built; so also the special bow and arrow. Invitations were sent to all the kings and noblemen, big and small in Bharatvarsh, including Krishna."

"And Krishna went there?"

"Yes, but more as a spectator and to see if the bait had worked," explained JT.

"It had, of course."

"Yes. Pandavas had heard about the contest where they were hiding as Brahmanas and headed for the venue."

"I think they had also had their share of adventure in the time gone by, with Bheem marrying Hidimba and then dealing with Bakasur," DK interjected.

"All duly spiced up by story tellers! But we won't let that detain us since our principal interest is in Krishna."

"Right."

"In the meantime, Yudhishthir had also figured out that they needed powerful allies to take on the Kauravas. In fact it is interesting how the same theme, *make friends and allies before entering real battle* runs through both our epics, Ramayan and Mahabharat. Therefore, coming for the *swayamvar* was a well thought out strategic move on the part of Pandavas too."

"Did Draupadi really taunt Karna at the *swayamvar*?" DK was curious.

"Ha Ha Ha...people have used a lot of vivid imagination to depict that interaction. Fact is Draupadi was her father's daughter, completely tuned in politically and fully aware of her role in her father's revenge ambitions. Clearly Karna, being Duryodhan's friend and thus sworn to be on Kaurav or Dronacharya's side, was a non-starter in her scheme of things.

So the 'he said-she said' is truly inconsequential in the larger picture. She would not have married him, no matter what."

"Yes and the larger picture is that Arjun won the *swayamvar*. But what about the five brothers marrying her?"

"That is an interesting one. And, from the perspective of 21st century with its emphasis on monogamy, it does look odd. In their anxiety to gloss over it quickly, early writers gave fanciful explanations of boons from the previous life or even the childish one of Kuntidevi saying 'divide the bhiksha' which the boys dutifully honoured. There is no need to be really coy about it, if one looks at the situation rationally."

"I am all ears," said DK.

"Remember, it was all political and Kuntidevi and her children were well aware of what the *swayamvar* was all about. Most versions have it that Krishna and Dhrishtadyumn followed the five brothers and Draupadi to their home where Krishna was overjoyed at his suspicions about the identity of the Brahmin boys being confirmed and at meeting his aunt Kuntidevi."

"Yes, I have read this."

"What may have happened next makes interesting speculation. It is entirely possible that Kuntidevi and Krishna concluded that one brother marrying a beauty and becoming the son-in-law of a rich and powerful king might sow seeds of dissension among the brothers. It is not an unusual situation even today. Even among sisters, if one were to marry a much richer man of higher social standing, differences start appearing soon enough."

"So true. It is human nature!"

"Exactly. It would have been obvious to Kuntidevi and to Krishna that unity among the brothers was Pandavas main strength and if it was jeopardised, all hope of getting justice in Hastinapur would be lost."

"That makes complete sense," said DK thoughtfully.

"It was clear from very early on that Yudhishthir had all qualities of being a great king and therefore Kuntidevi and Krishna figured out this solution of all five brothers marrying Draupadi. Remember, polyandry was not unknown in ancient India, it had been practiced in the Kinnaur region of today's Himachal Pradesh for ages. It was also not too far away from where Pandu Maharaj's *ashram* was, where the Pandavas were born, so Kuntidevi was surely aware of it."

"Wasn't that also the region where Pandavas were later to spend some of their exile period?"

"Yes, it was," said JT.

"Hmm. Who do you think thought of this out-of-the-box solution? Kuntidevi or Krishna?"

"It hardly matters who did; women are generally much smarter than men about matters relating to relationships, so it could have been Kuntidevi. But given that Krishna had already demonstrated his ability to come up with creative solutions to tough problems...take your pick."

"I think that is a good note on which to take our delayed lunch break. The subject was so engrossing, I lost track of time."

"Okay here we are. Time for some Coimbatori preparations at this Southern Delight Restaurant," said JT as he brought *nandighosh* to a halt in the parking lot.

***

"There should be a ban on *Payasam* as good as we just had. I have to fight the temptation to get my forty winks, but I can't wait to take the story forward," said DK, as they got into *nandighosh* again post lunch.

"A dialogue with fellow passengers is any way recommended for those behind the steering wheel," replied JT as he took his customary driver's seat. "Especially after a heavy meal," he added with a smile.

"So tell me, what exactly changed in the lives of Pandavas after their marriage to Draupadi?"

"Politically, that marriage changed the entire landscape of Bharatvarsh. Pandavas were no longer just five poverty stricken non-entities to be brushed aside easily. In Hastinapur, Duryodhan, Shakuni and their cohorts were shocked that Pandavas had escaped from their clutches in Varnavrat and Lakshagrah but they were in no position to say much without exposing their dastardly plot. Elders like Dhritrashtra also had no option but to profess their relief at Pandavas being alive. Moreover, now that Pandavas had a powerful king like Drupad in their corner, they could not be trifled with. Not to forget Krishna, whose exploits had already earned him an aura few kings possessed. Not really surprising then that Dhritrashtra and the court elders agreed to divide the kingdom. Pandavas got Khandavprasth."

"Was it a fair division?"

"Hardly, but then it would not have been really reasonable to expect Hastinapur, where all the elders had resided all their lives, to be given to Pandavas."

"So how did Khandavprasth become Indraprastha?"

"No overnight magic this time too, I am afraid. Krishna summoned his trusted Vishwakarma. Since the team had already created one masterpiece in Dwarka, creating a second one was not such a big challenge. It probably took a couple of years."

"But many writers have said it happened instantly!" protested DK.

"Writers who wrote thousands or hundreds of years later. In any case, to those who were seeing this level of construction for the first time, it was nothing short of magic and it may have seemed like an instant."

"So what really happened in Indraprastha once Pandavas had settled in?"

"This was perhaps the best time of the Pandavas lives with not too many tragedies. And that is why, perhaps, it has not attracted as much attention of writers as other periods have. That is the way writers pick and choose. Many happy incidents took place during this period of maybe 15-20 years."

"Tell me a few please," requested DK.

"Well, to start with they all had very fruitful family lives during this phase. Draupadi had her five children from the five brothers; however, she wasn't the only one. All the Pandav brothers had other marriages and children during this phase; Yudhishthir married an apsara, Bheem married Jalandhara, in addition to Hidimba, who he had married long back, Nakul married Anumit and Sahadeva got into matrimony with Vijay."

"What about Krishna and Arjun?" asked DK.

"Krishna was busy strengthening Dwarka during this period. He married Satyabhama, Satrajit's daughter, which put an end to the Syamantaka jewel saga. After Satrajit's death Satyabhama and through her, Krishna, inherited that precious jewel anyway."

"And Arjun?"

"Arjun went on his country-wide *yatra* as a penance for intruding on Yudhishthir and Draupadi's private moments and ended up marrying thrice, including notably to Krishna's sister Subhadra. Bheem's bravery we all know about but Nakul and Sahadeva were brave generals in their own rights and helped expand the kingdom in different directions. But most important of all, Yudhishthir being a just and capable king, took his kingdom to new heights. It soon became the premier kingdom in all of Bharatvarsh."

"Aah, the root cause of neighbour's envy!" DK interjected.

JT laughed. "Yes, we will come to that. Actually, it was only a matter of time before someone suggested to Yudhishthir that it was time for him to hold a Rajsuya Yagna."

"What was that?"

"It was in effect a proclamation that the king was god's representative on earth and established his pre-eminence among kings."

"Clearly an important step up."

"Yes, so Yudhishthir decided to consult Krishna on this. This is where Krishna once again showed his command over lateral as well as strategic thinking."

"How was that?" DK asked.

"He pointed out to Yudhishthir that it would be inappropriate to have a Rajsuya Yagna while Jarasandha was still in harness. Jarasandha had 86 kings captive in his custody and was planning a big *yagna* the moment he reached 100. Any such happening would undermine any other king's claims to pre-eminence."

"That sounds reasonable."

"It was and Yudhishthir understood it. The problem was that Jarasandha had huge forces which were practically unbeatable."

"Quite a conundrum."

"That is where Krishna's strategic insights shone again. He knew that, to paraphrase a modern truism, 'God is usually on the side of the larger armies'. He, therefore, ruled out military-to-military test of strength. He also knew that Jarasandha was a vain man, proud of his wrestling skills. In Bheem, the Pandavas had a physically unbeatable hero and Krishna capitalised on it."

"I remember reading about a long drawn wrestling bout."

"Yes, it was. Krishna, Arjun and Bheem sneaked into Jarasandha's capital and lured him into a one-on-one bout with the opponent of his choice. By this time their identities were known and vain man that he was, Jarasandha chose Bheem as his opponent. Eventually, after a long bout lasting many days, Jarasandha was killed," explained JT.

"What about all the added bits: his being torn into two parts and thrown into opposite directions?"

"Yes, legend has it that he was born to the two wives of Magadh King Brihadrath, half to each, and the parts later came together thanks to a *rakshasi*. The story is that he could only be killed by being torn apart. As I said earlier, how much of all this is *masala* added by later writers is hard to know. In any case, these are matters of Dwapar Yuga, we do not know enough of the rules of the game then to be judgemental. I am quite happy taking the end result as the death of Jarasandha and moving on. In the process of clearing the way for Yudhishthir's *yagna*, Krishna had eliminated his own bugbear, someone who had posed a threat all his life. Few incidents demonstrate Krishna's capacity for killing two birds with one strategic stone as clearly as this one does."

"Yes, I can see that. So what happened next?"

"They freed all the kings who, of course, swore fidelity to Yudhishthir. They then installed Jarasandha's son Sahadeva — not to be confused with the Pandav of the same name — on the throne after he had agreed to become a vassal of Maharaj Yudhishthir."

"That must have cleared the way for Yudhishthir's *yagna* completely."

"Yes, but Jarasandha's death has much greater significance. Jarasandha-Krishna rivalry was known to all of Bharatvarsh. Many had even dubbed Krishna *'Ranchoddas'* over his tactics of avoiding frontal combat with Jarasandha or his forces. It was only after Jarasandha's death that the brilliance of Krishna's strategy and tactics became evident to everyone. Krishna had waited and waited patiently, till the moment was right and when he judged it to be so, struck fast and hard through Bheem. We can be sure that the entire Bharatvarsh, including the sceptics and fence-sitters till then, were totally awestruck by the development," pointed out JT.

"Hmm...yes, it must have been so and it clears up several aspects. We tend to gloss over known incidents without spending much time in understanding their all-round ripple effects."

"Not just ripple, the impact must have been close to a tidal effect. It gave a boost to those who had started ascribing divinity to Krishna ever since he overcame Kansa."

"And of course it paved the way for Yudhishthir's *yagna*."

"It did, but nothing came easily to Pandavas."

"Why, what happened now?" DK asked, puzzled.

"Oh it was a massive occasion. Kings and royalty from all over Bharatvarsh came. It was a truly huge celebration. And among the invitees was Shishupal, King of Chedi."

"Erstwhile competitor of Krishna for Rukmini's hand?"

"Yes. Now, as part of the *yagna*, Yudhishthir had to nominate someone for *agrapuja*, or the first guest of honour. Usually one would have expected Yudhishthir to choose Bhishma Pitamah, the venerable grandsire of the Kuru clan or perhaps Guru Dronacharya. Instead, he chose Krishna."

"Why did he do that?" wondered DK.

"It was not an impulsive decision surely. Yudhishthir was an intelligent man and he must have weighed his options. Krishna had intervened thrice in Pandavas' lives and each time his intervention had proved decisive. First, during Draupadi *swayamvar* and then getting Draupadi to marry the five brothers thus eliminating a possible cause of rift among them; second, in extracting Khandavprasth as family settlement from the Kuru elders and third, in figuring out how to get rid of Jarasandha, the main obstacle in the path to the *yagna*."

"And the elders?"

"Yudhishthir was sober, not given to angry diatribes or loud displays of displeasure, but he must have felt slighted by Bhishma and others. First, none of them, except Vidur who had limited authority, did much to rein in Duryodhan or anticipate attempts on their lives; second, whatever Yudhishthir and his brothers had managed to achieve was largely despite, and not because of, the family elders. It is very likely that with the gesture of inviting Krishna for the *agrapuja*, Yudhishthir also sent a message to the elders."

"Did they show any resentment?"

"Not them, they were a polished lot. But Shishupal did. He objected in strong words and wondered aloud if Yudhishthir had taken leave of his senses to invite a cowherd for the honour of *agrapuja* when there were so many illustrious seniors present."

"All the frustration of losing Rukmini came out!" observed DK.

"Yes and the language was extremely abusive too, directed mainly at Krishna. Krishna heard him out patiently and when he had had enough, decapitated Shishupal with his Sudarshan Chakra."

"After he had completed his hundred sins?" probed DK.

"Yes, there is that story too. Actually, Shishupal was the son of Srutashubha, a sister of Vasudev, exactly the way Pandavas were the sons of Kuntidevi, another sister of Vasudev. He was a cousin of Krishna just like the Pandavas were. There is the story that Krishna had promised Srutashubha, his aunt, that he will spare Shishupal's life till he commits a hundred offences. But like in Jarasandha's case, it is best that we accept the end result, Shishupal's death, and move on."

"The *yagna* was completed thereafter?"

"Yes and a very significant milestone in Yudhishthir's life it was to be. But equally, in the life of Krishna and, in a manner of speaking, in the life of Bharatvarsh itself."

"How so?" DK was puzzled.

"Look at it this way. Krishna was not even the king of Dwarka; that position was still held by Ugrasen, Krishna's grandfather. And Dwarka itself was really a small town, nothing compared to the mighty kingdoms of Indraprastha or Hastinapur or Magadh or Panchal. And yet Krishna had demonstrated that with his strategies he could dominate the political discourse within the entire Bharatvarsh, that without him, Yudhishthir could not have become a *samrat*. This was indirectly acknowledged by Yudhishthir, by according Krishna the honour of *agrapuja*."

"Well, yes."

"Bear in mind that all these events were also shaping Krishna's world view. He learnt from his encounters with evil, whether in the form of Kansa or Jarasandha, and he learnt from the political manoeuvring in Draupadi *swayamvar* or the establishment of Indraprastha or in Yudhishthir becoming a *samrat*. You could say this was the preparation of a 'Grandmaster in the Making', for bigger tests were yet to come."

"I think we can leave them for tomorrow then. Bigger tests may be yet to come but Coimbatore has already arrived.

Lots of food for thought today; why don't we call it a day here at this Southern Star Petrol Pump and try and continue tomorrow?"

"Sounds great," said JT as he *nandighosh* eased into a parking slot.

❑❑❑

CHAPTER 7

Clash of the Titans

"Problems, problems?" queried JT gently as *nandighosh* began its journey the next day.

"You are a mind reader. Two of them actually," DK said adjusting his seat-belt.

"Go on."

"Yet another detour. The owner of the Saree Emporium in Coimbatore showed us his saree collection late last evening as planned."

"And the lady did not approve any," JT said with a knowing smile.

"No no, that part is done, no problem. But while the owner was showing the sarees on the video call, the ladies also noticed something else in the background: a beautiful bell metal lamp and an exquisite brass statuette of Goddess Laxmi. Meera is very fond of such artefacts. On enquiring we were told that the best place to buy them is in Madurai. The owner immediately phoned and arranged for a 25 per cent discount to be given to us. Since I expect to be going to USA soon, I might as well carry them myself."

"Okay, so off we go to Madurai first; another extra day is still no big deal. What was the other thing?"

"They are to visit Meera's doctor today and that always makes me tense."

"Relax, everything will be okay."

"Let us get back to where we were. The distraction helps me. So what happened after the Rajsuya Yagna? Everything seemed to be hunky dory at that point."

"Actually, it wasn't," said JT thoughtfully. "While one's genuine well-wishers are truly happy at a celebration of one's progress, it often stirs up other emotions in some who may not be so well disposed."

"Duryodhan and his friends we know about...who were the others?" DK was curious.

"King Shalva for one. He was a close friend of Shishupal and was very upset when his friend was killed. Since Krishna was away in Indraprastha, he thought the opportunity was perfect and attacked Dwarka."

"Politics as usual."

"Of course, there is never an end to it. Krishna's son Pradyumna and others defended valiantly, but the moment Krishna got word of it, he naturally rushed back to Dwarka."

"Even if he had made good speed, it would have taken five or six days at least."

"More probably, because he was challenged on the way by Dantavakra."

"New name. Who was he?" DK was puzzled.

"The King of Karusha, a small kingdom. He was also in the Jarasandha, Shishupal camp. According to Vishnu Purana and some editions of Bhagvad Purana...."

"Showing off!"

"Ha ha, no, I try not to but since it is a new name, I thought I should tell you where it comes from. Anyway, he was supposed to be another of Krishna's cousins, son of Vriddhashraman and Shrutadevi, who was Kuntidevi's sister. He had the exact same relationship with Krishna as Shishupal did."

"And this Dantavakra challenged Krishna on the way to Dwarka?"

"Yes. The idea may have been to delay his arrival in Dwarka while Shalva plundered it. He was successful to an extent but paid the price with his life when he was killed by Krishna in a mace fight."

"That makes him the second cousin that Krishna killed in quick succession."

"Alright, so what happened when Krishna reached Dwarka?" asked DK.

"It took some time but he defeated Shalva. What happened in Hastinapur and Indraprastha once Krishna had left after the Rajsuya Yagna was more important in terms of lasting significance."

"What happened? Of course the dice game!"

"Correct. Duryodhan and his advisors, mainly Shakuni, decided on a devious plot and invited Yudhishthir for a game of dice."

"I know why it happened. Draupadi had taunted Duryodhan '*andhe ka beta andha*'," DK said with complete confidence.

"Ha ha ha... you watch too many TV serials."

"Why isn't that what happened?"

"No way. According to authorities like K M Ganguli — you know he was the first to translate Mahabharat into English in the 19th century, right? — Draupadi wasn't even present when Duryodhan met with all those accidents in the palace of illusions. Yes, Bheem and the younger Pandavas enjoyed Duryodhan's discomfiture and Duryodhan, in turn, added a lot of *masala* while reporting the Pandavas wealth and luxury to Dhritrashtra. That is when the bit about Draupadi and the court ladies taunting him very likely got added, to underline his humiliation and to convince Dhritrashtra about the need for revenge."

"You are saying Draupadi did not taunt Duryodhan?" DK was puzzled.

"Not in the manner popular imagination would have it. Look, she was a fiery lady, so it is entirely possible that she may have shown off the Pandavas wealth and accomplishments in some pointed manner to rub their cousins' noses in the dust. But no serious student really buys this '*andhe ka beta...*' business."

"No shortage of *masala* in India, can't really blame TV producers for adding some. Is that why Dhritrashtra gave permission for the game of dice?"

"Yes. And the question which troubles many, although it is inconsequential really, is why did Yudhishthir accept the invitation?"

"Yes please, why? And why is it inconsequential?" persisted DK.

"Many scholars have given many answer to the first why and the most reasonable seems to be that Yudhishthir had been cautioned about the consequences of hostility with his cousins. He, therefore, went out of the way to avoid giving offence and accepted the invitation. Or possibly he was just fond of gambling with dice and Duryodhan cleverly played on his weakness."

"And why is it inconsequential?" DK wondered.

JT replied thoughtfully. "Well, envy is a strange master and the opulence of the Pandavas seen at the Rajsuya Yagna had probably set in motion a chain of events with its own momentum. Once Duryodhan had decided to avenge his real or imagined humiliation, the dice game was only incidental. If Yudhishthir had turned the invitation down, Duryodhan would have found some other reason and with a crook like Shakuni advising him, there would have been no shortage of options. Remember the man had even found ways to procure the poisonous *nightshade* from shady sources when Duryodhan wanted to poison Bheem decades ago."

"So Yudhishthir accepted the invitation and lost the game. What really happened after that?"

"That something disgraceful happened is clear. Draupadi was dragged into the court wearing a single piece of cloth, as was the custom then, when a lady was menstruating."

"Disgusting indeed! She did protest strongly and with so much logic."

"The happenings then in the Hastinapur Raj Sabha are extremely dramatic with lots of potential for arguments about whether a wife indeed has an independent existence or is she the property of the husband to be staked in a wager and whether in a marriage under polyandry, one husband could brush away the claims of other husbands so easily. No wonder so much has been written about it."

"And then that fiend Dushhasan attempted to strip her when she prayed to Krishna who came to rescue..." DK said with confidence.

"That is the most popular version, yes, and a strong pillar on which the case for Krishna's divinity rests."

"There are other versions?" asked DK, surprised.

JT smiled. "Your surprise does not surprise me. The TV visuals of endless sarees being provided to Draupadi with special computer graphics were truly powerful, but were probably very distant from whatever might have really happened. Ved

Vyas himself has said 'Dharma' saved Draupadi from shame but left it unclear as to who or what he meant by 'Dharma'. It could be Vidur, it could be Yudhishthir or it could be something else."

"That is a new twist. Any other versions?" DK persisted.

"Yes, definitely. In Shiv Purana, it is a boon given by Sage Durvasa which saves her. In the Sarala Mahabharat, an Odiya version, it is the Sun God who rescues her. But a simpler explanation might be the straight forward interpretation of 'Dharma' mentioned by Ved Vyas as 'proper conduct'. Draupadi conducted herself properly and argued her case very persuasively so she was rewarded by Dhritrashtra himself, perhaps with some nudging from Vidur, also referred to sometimes as 'Dharma' because he was seen as justice personified. Dhritrashtra effectively cancelled the result of the game and restored the status-quo-ante. Very hard to think of another logical reason for Dhritrashtra to do so."

"Oh yes, a lot of people forget that part. There do seem to be a number of alternative explanations of the incident other than Krishna intervening magically."

"We must remember that at this crucial time Krishna was engaged in the campaign against Shalva, so fanciful explanations involving him, while being very appealing emotionally, are really thin on logic and likelihood. Of course, if we accept the divine dimension in Krishna, this incident is easily explained. But then troublesome questions arise as to why it took so long to subdue Jarasandha, where was the need to rope in Bheem for that and so on."

"Hmm. What happened next?"

"Duryodhan chastised his father for having thrown away a victory and prevailed upon him to invite the Pandavas again for a game, this time with fixed stake of Kingdom plus

12 years of exile followed by a year of *adnyaatvaas* or remaining incognito."

"Surely Yudhishthir should have resisted playing the game a second time! Surely his brothers and Draupadi had had enough of the humiliation and tried to stop him!"

"They did and failed. That was one time Yudhishthir badly needed Krishna's sage advice. It was not available and so he accepted the invitation. Clearly by this time his attachment to the game had also started overpowering his otherwise fine sense of right and wrong."

"Yes, any addiction seems to impair judgement and often common sense."

"What followed was predictable. Shakuni won again on behalf of Duryodhan and the Pandavas had to leave for their 12 years of exile as agreed."

"What a terrible outcome!" exclaimed DK, feeling the pain.

"Yes. When the news reached Krishna — by that time he had subdued Shalva — he rushed to meet them. Pandavas with their huge entourage had barely progressed beyond crossing the river Ganga at that point."

"Did he fire Yudhishthir?"

"He did not and there is a very important lesson even in that. What is past is past, there is little point in looking backwards and thinking about what should have been done. Instead, Krishna immediately got down to practical matters."

"Exactly the way he dealt with every crisis in his life. Do whatever is necessary."

"Yes, that could have been his magic mantra. He sent all the other Pandav wives with their children to their respective *maikas* and he himself took Subhadra and the child Abhimanyu with him to Dwarka," explained JT.

"Well, Draupadi may have got her *thali* soon for taking care of Pandavas appetites during the exile. But for our appetites, we may need to stop at some good place soon."

"This Southern Delight looks attractive enough and appropriately enough, their billboard also advertises a Deluxe *Thali*. Let us take a break here," said JT and *nandighosh* came to a smooth halt.

***

"So what about the wonderful stories of Draupadi's *thali* and Durvasa Rishi with Krishna again turning out to be Draupadi's saviour?" asked DK as *nandighosh* resumed its journey post-lunch. Clearly the delicious *thali* they just had was still playing on his mind.

"Fun story. How Durvasa Rishi, known for his temper, came unannounced and expected Draupadi to feed him and his followers; how Krishna turned up mysteriously, evidently had one grain of rice still sticking to the magical *thali* after Draupadi had washed up post lunch and that was enough to satiate the learned *rishi* and his followers!"

"Sounds fantastic."

"Yes and surely one of the many additions to the original Ved Vyas composition. Ved Vyas had written only 8,800 verses originally, what we have now is over one lakh of them. Most of the additions are harmless and great fun to read. But not necessarily of much significance."

"What were the really significant incidents which took place in the 12 years of *vanvaas* of the Pandavas? And what did Krishna do in the meantime?" asked DK.

"Krishna focussed on Dwarka and, as and when the opportunity rose, built goodwill for Pandavas across Bharatvarsh. He did meet them a few times like at Prabhas, with Balaram and

Satyaki when the Pandavas, minus Arjun, were on a *teerth yatra* or when Markandeya Muni visited them. That was when Arjun was away in search of special weapons, which was probably the most important thing that happened to Pandavas during the 12 year period."

"Oh, I thought many adventures took place."

"That is a 21st century mind romanticising forest dwelling! But yes, that 12 year period was practically a non-stop education for Pandavas. They visited many *ashrams* of learned *rishis* and *munis*. With each one Yudhishthir had long discussions and we may be sure all that went into making Yudhishthir the great king that he was to become eventually."

"Wasn't he tempted to go to war with Kauravas at any time during the period of exile?" DK asked.

"Look at it this way, Yudhishthir did play by the book in going into exile for 12 years, and not declaring war immediately or at any time during those years, as Bheem and Arjun often suggested. At the same time he was being pragmatic. He realised that apart from being the honourable thing to do, it was also very practical. When there were *Maharathis* of the calibre of Bhishma, Drona, Ashwatthama and Karna in the opposing camp, caution was advisable. At least till they had got allies and matching weaponry issues sorted out."

"Let us get back to Arjun's search for special weapons. His *tapasya* on mount Indrakila, his encounter with Shiva in the form of a hunter are well known."

"Yes, almost all versions of Mahabharat describe that Arjun got the Pashupatastra from Shiva after that. Besides, he also got celestial weapons from others *devas* like Varun, Kubera and Yama."

"One thing I haven't understood about this part. I do not recall Arjun using the Pashupatastra any time during the

Mahabharat war. So what was the point of going to all the trouble to acquire it?" DK was genuinely puzzled.

"Yes, the Pashupatastra, described as the most powerful of all divine weapons, was not used during Mahabharat war at all. It was indeed used by Arjun, but elsewhere. Most Mahabharat versions fail to connect the related dots, though many scholarly works do. Let me simplify the explanation for you.

After Arjun got the weapons from the *devas*, Indra Dev's pilot Matali took Arjun to Amravati, the capital of Devlok. It transpired that *devas* and asuras called *nivatkavachas* were engaged in a running battle. The *devas* were struggling because the latter had a boon that they could be defeated only by a human. That was the main reason Arjun's father Indra Dev had brought Arjun to Devlok, to fight on behalf of *devas*. In that battle, described ever so beautifully in the serious works I mentioned, Arjun is said to have used both, the *Pashupatastra* and the *Vajra,* which he got from Indra Dev, to destroy the *nivatkavachas.*"

"Aah, now I get it!" exclaimed DK.

"Of course, as always, access to specialised weapons was severely restricted and that really is the key takeaway of the story."

"Explain please."

"See, a very good case can be made that leadership among communities or among nations is more directly related to a country's strength in weapons technology rather than to its wealth in gold and diamonds or art or architecture or knowledge of sciences or any other parameter. When men first tamed horses, the horsemen became the leaders and so on throughout the ages. Swords, spears, bow and arrow, gunpowder, rifles, cannons, they all conferred leadership of communities or races to those groups which mastered them first. The 15th to the 19th century belonged to European nations mainly on the strength of their naval technologies and guns. The swords and spears of locals in different parts of the world were no match for the guns and cannons of the European powers. Even countries with a lot of other wealth could not withstand the onslaught."

DK absorbed it all for a minute. "I can see the connection. And, all leaders guarded their knowledge of weapons technology zealously."

"Yes, of course. People may think Non-Proliferation Treaty or NPT on nuclear weapons is a new idea but the concept is as old as mankind itself."

"Okay so Arjun got the precious weapons, which sort of balanced the scales with Kauravas."

"Correct. And the time had come for Pandavas to spend a year incognito in King Virat's court."

"I love the Virat Parv but one thing troubles me. How did Yudhishthir get appointed as an advisor to King Virat on the strength of the claim that he had been not just an advisor to Maharaj Yudhishthir on political matters but also his dice playing partner? I would have thought that such a claim would hardly have added any credibility to his Resume'!"

"Ha ha, true. That would have remained a loose end if Maharshi Vyas had not tied it up neatly by narrating about the Pandavas meeting Muni Brihadaswa during their *vanvas*. He was the master of the arcane *Akshahridaya*, the art, maths and science of playing with dice. He taught Yudhishthir thoroughly and after that Yudhishthir was really unbeatable at the game."

"Pity they did not meet up before the infamous gambling match," observed DK.

"Some things may be destined to happen the way they did."

"What is fantastic about the Virat Parv is that so many exciting episodes took place. I got goosebumps reading about the way Bheem killed Kichak, who took undue interest in the queen's maid Sairandhri, Draupadi in disguise. And then the way Arjun rendered all the Kaurav warriors unconscious and stole away their clothes with Prince Uttar Kumar as his partner at the end of the *adnyaatvaas* had me jumping out of my chair in excitement."

"That episode tickles the child in each of us," JT smiled and said. "That was Arjun using the *Sammohiniastra* or the weapon for hypnotising he had got from Kubera for the first time. But, of far greater and lasting importance, are the events which took place after their identities were disclosed to King Virat."

"Yes," DK was serious now. "King Virat suggested that Arjun marry his daughter Princess Uttara. And then Duryodhan sent a messenger asking the Pandavas to get back to the forest, since according to him, the period of their *adnyaatvaas* was not over yet."

"Laughable claim as Bhishma Pitamah was the first to point out. And, Arjun suggested to King Virat that Princess Uttara marry his son Abhimanyu. That makes it obvious that Pandavas seeking refuge in Matsya kingdom was well-planned. It was never meant to be a one year hideaway, it was always meant to be the opening move in assembling allies, who could one day help Pandavas face the Kauravas in a war."

"Makes sense," remarked DK.

"In a very short time there was an assembly of the foremost of Pandava sympathisers in Uplayva, the city which King Virat offered the Pandavas as their temporary base. Krishna came with Balaram, Satyaki and of course Subhadra and Abhimanyu; King Drupad came with his two sons, Shikhandi and Dhrishtadyumn. And while the wedding of Abhimanyu and Princess Uttara was celebrated with suitable pomp and show, it was clear that the end game of the real contest in Bharatvarsh was about to begin."

"I remember there was much going back and forth of messengers, including a respected senior from Drupad's court and Sanjay from the Kauravas side."

"To no avail of course. And then finally Krishna volunteered to go himself."

"Why did he do that?" DK asked.

"That is a very important question and also one of the most important clues in trying to understand Krishna. There are at least three good reasons why Krishna took it upon himself to go to Hastinapur on a mediation mission."

"Let's hear them," DK was keen to know.

"Firstly, once his objective was clear, Krishna always studied people closely, whether friends or opponents. He had studied Kansa and the political situation in Mathura before the wrestling match; he had studied Jarasandha well and it was only when his SWOT analysis revealed the chink in Jarasandha's armour that he figured out a way to bait him into a one-on-one bout with Bheem. Krishna was also clear in his assessment that Kauravs represented an evil which was bad for the *praja* as a whole and had to be tackled firmly. He did not want Yudhishthir to go into that den of vice where who knew what trap might await him, and so chose to volunteer for the task himself. He was no mere messenger though; by this time his stature was such that everyone, including the Kauravas, knew that any commitment made by him would be honoured by the Pandavas," elaborated JT.

"Second?"

"The second reason was the short term goal of tilting the odds towards Pandavas, if his assessment that there could be no compromise with a belligerent Duryodhan was proven correct. To that end, Krishna meticulously planned out what he was going to say to each of the key players. If war turned out to be inevitable, as he suspected it might be, the earlier the process of weakening the enemy started, the better it would be. And creating dissensions among the enemy ranks is a time tested method towards that."

"And the third?"

"The third was a long term view. By this time of course Krishna knew that he was venerated by many across Bharatvarsh as an *avataar*. His deeds were spoken of with awe. He was celebrated in song and dance and very likely in a few temples too. Krishna recognised that no matter what happened from there on, his role would be scrutinised minutely by scholars and sages for a long time in the future. He wanted posterity to be clear about him, that he had tried his best to avoid a human slaughter of monumental proportions that he could see coming if his peace mission failed. For that it was essential for him to go personally, and make all efforts despite his personal assessment that Duryodhan had gone beyond the point where reasonable peace would have been possible."

"And Duryodhan with his angry rejection of the most modest five villages proposal with 'not even an area equal to a pinhead' buried all chances of peace," DK said.

"*Vinaash kaley viparit buddhi*—when your destruction beckons, your reason misguides you. Yes that diatribe alone puts the blame for the war squarely at Duryodhan's doorstep."

"But what about the others?"

"Bhishma, Drona, even Dhritrashtra tried to reason with Duryodhan, Gandharidevi was also roped in but Duryodhan was too far gone. What it did do is to underline the tensions and shades of differences among all of them and these can be seen in the uneasy relationships during the war itself."

"What about Karna?"

"Karna was part of the coterie along with Shakuni and Dushhasan which kept on egging Duryodhan. But Krishna took care to neutralise Karna to a considerable extent by revealing to him the secret of his birth; that he was Kuntidevi's son."

"That must have jolted Karna!"

"Of course it did. And Karna kept out of the first half of the war somehow, till Bhishma Pitamah was the Commander-in-Chief, ostensibly because of some spat with him."

"At any rate, one big *Maharathi* on the Kaurav side had been neutralised for a while but how did Krishna come to know the secret of Karn's birth?" DK asked logically.

"Good question. Most accounts treat it lightly because once the premise of his divinity is accepted, there is no need for such questions. But a logical, reasonable, alternate explanation stares us in the face. He stayed at Vidur's house during the peace mission and Kuntidevi was also staying there. What would be more natural than a mother, keen to avoid a head-on clash between her sons, confiding her long-held secret to Krishna? After all, he was the one person who represented a slim ray of hope for her of avoiding that particular calamity," JT pointed out.

"Ok, so Kunti told Krishna who in turn revealed it to Karna. The mission was then successful despite being unsuccessful!" said DK in wonderment.

"Actually, it looks like a flawlessly executed plan, no matter how one looks at it."

DK looked outside the window. Darkness had set in.

"It has been a long day and we hardly noticed that we were stuck in a traffic jam for an hour since the discussion was so enlightening."

"Let us halt at the petrol pump ahead and continue our discussion tomorrow."

"Yes, the stage is set for the final clash of the titans. And just in time too! Hopefully by tomorrow evening we should reach Srirangam."

❑❑❑

CHAPTER 8

Dharmakshetre Kurukshetre

"Why the late start today?" asked JT as they got into *nandighosh* later than their normal routine.

"Two things. One you know, the other you don't."

"Okay, the good news-bad news thing. Alright, tell me the part I know," said JT as *nandighosh* swung on to the main road.

"The buying of the special bell lamps and the Laxmi statuette was a very satisfying experience. Brilliant pieces of art, very reasonably priced."

"And the part I don't know?"

"Meera's friend also seemed to have liked them very much, so I had to order a couple of pieces more which took a little time being delivered this morning."

"That's why the delay. Hardly matters, it's a shorter journey today; it gives me time to work out my plans for later. Southern India has always had some brilliant metal workers and I am glad it is getting recognised," said JT.

"There is something more that I haven't told you," DK smiled like a naughty boy. "Four days ago I forgot to take my BP meds, but my morning-evening BP levels remained fine. Since then I have deliberately omitted them and the levels still remained fine."

"That is fantastic, but it is better to avoid such adventures without consulting doctors," cautioned JT.

"I know, but our discussions have been so soothing. So many cobwebs in my mind have got cleared. Or it could be just the relief of getting out of an enclosed space from Covid struck Mumbai and inhaling some fresh countryside air. Anyway, the impact of Covid seems to be much lesser on highways."

"Sure it has been a relief. And some of the countryside has been so picturesque. A sight for sore eyes."

"But no sight for sore eyes greeted Arjun or Krishna when the two armies faced each other on the battlefield of Kurukshetra."

"Yes, the moment of reckoning was at hand and Arjun developed cold feet," JT said.

"That is a surprise really, for such a gifted warrior, perhaps the most accomplished *Maharathi* of his time to start having second thoughts at such a crucial time!"

"It can happen to the best of us. And he was in a way really the best of us. It is essentially the same feeling many get when standing at some cross roads, when the stakes are very high and every decision seems problematic."

"I can see the moment more clearly. The thought that *this* could be the most crucial moment of my life can make a lot of people nervous and Arjun seems to have been no exception."

"Not just *the* crucial moment of one person's life, what Arjun faced was *the* crucial moment in the lives of his brothers, his family, the kingdom, the Kuru dynasty and, in hindsight, even mankind itself. The burden was heavy and for a moment Arjun was shaken up," explained JT.

"Good thing Krishna was there to restore his equilibrium."

"As it turned out, not just for Arjun but for mankind itself."

"Yes, I am eager to move on to Gita."

"Hundreds of scholars have interpreted Gita in so many different ways. There is very little that needs to be said about its contents."

"True. Its basic messages of 'Do Your Duty', 'Detach Yourself From The Result' are too well known to need repetition."

"Well known, yes, but not easy to practise. The challenge arises because each of us has multiple identities and duties. You may be a son, father, husband, employee or an owner of a business and in the larger context, a citizen of your city, state or country. Each of these roles has a set of duties attached to it. What happens when one set of 'duties' comes into conflict with another?"

"Like a Venn diagram you mean. There are N number of intersecting 'Duty Circles'?"

"Which may or may not have a common area. Something like that, yes. Your boss wants you to travel for some critical work and your father at home needs urgent medical attention. What do you do?"

"One needs to prioritise, depending on the situation," said DK thoughtfully.

"Exactly. That is a judgement call and that is where many fail. Even within Mahabharat, practically every character is found falling short on some occasion or the other."

"Explain please."

"Take Dhritrashtra for example. He was completely aware on many occasions when Duryodhan was in the wrong. In fact Vidur cautioned him on practically every occasion, and yet, he faltered while exercising his judgement among what he thought were his duties as a Father and his duties as the King. Similarly, Bhishma Pitamah. In the *vastraharan* episode, he failed in exercising his judgement correctly while choosing between his sworn duty towards Hastinapur and his natural duty as the patriarch of the Kuru family. Practically, all the characters in Mahabharat were confronted with decision-making dilemmas and found wanting at some point."

"So true."

"There are a couple of exceptions, but we can talk about them later. Gita, in many ways, is a guide on how to exercise judgement when facing a conflict between two or more perceived duties. What is even more interesting though is that if you look at the central messages of different chapters, it is not too difficult to imagine how Krishna's own life experiences may have shaped those."

"That sounds new. Explain please," DK requested.

"For example, early on in his life during the Indra Puja incident we talked about the other day, Krishna realised the importance of fearlessly following logical thinking without worrying too much about where it led to. Even if it was against everything that the society around him believed in. That could well be the reason why the first chapter of Gita underlines that *'Wrong thinking may lie at the root of all problems in life'*."

"Oh, never thought of it that way!"

"Krishna was doing a very delicate job, hand-holding Arjun and getting him back on track to do what needed to be done. In the process the entire message in Gita is so effectively and beautifully put together that it has inspired mankind for thousands of years."

"Timeless really."

"Exactly but interestingly enough, it means different things to different people at different stages of life. For the same person, the meaning changes as per the context. If you read it at 20, you may take away one message, if you read it at 40 another one and yet another one at 60."

DK thought it over. "Never occurred to me. But it is true, now that I think of it."

"Think for a moment of how Krishna defeated Chanoor fearlessly," said JT.

"He had youth, physical skill and enthusiasm, of course."

"Plus he had the knowledge that the people of Mathura were fed up of Kansa's rule and will not rise in Kansa or Chanoor's favour. Priceless foreknowledge must have given him enormous confidence going into the ring."

"Second chapter of Gita," DK said as light dawned on him and he connected the dots, '*Right knowledge is the solution to all our problems.*'

"That's the point I was coming to. Each such nugget of wisdom that Krishna learnt in life was tested and reconfirmed by later incidents too."

"Yes, he had the foreknowledge, indeed took pains to acquire it, about Jarasandha's vanity."

"We need not talk about every chapter, but I would encourage you to have a fresh look at Gita in the light of Krishna's life and see how his life experiences translated into the specific points he made to Arjun."

"I was already thinking of Chapter 7. 'Live what you learn' But that is exactly what Krishna seems to have done himself. Put into action whatever he had learnt till that point in life without fear or hesitation."

"Yes, the emphasis on *action* is important in understanding Krishna."

"And chapter 13 about *detachment.* Such a masterly concept once you understand it."

" '*Keep doing what is right in the circumstances without worrying about the result*'. In most cases the result also depends on other factors such as what others do or some external factors, which you have no control over, so why waste time thinking of the result? So simple, so elegant, saves so much time and needless heartburn," said JT.

"It is easy to see why Arjun was totally mesmerised by the end."

"In any case, it put his mind at ease and he again picked up his *Gandeev Dhanushya*."

"That seems to be a good point to break for lunch at the next decent restaurant. The chat this morning has been so revealing and has cleared up so many of my doubts, but I need time to digest the fresh takeaways. Along with some delightful *Rasam* I have started fancying."

***

"There is something very special about coming towards the end of a journey," said DK, as their travel resumed after lunch. "Especially if it has been a great journey, like this one has been. One doesn't want it to end and yet there is the eagerness to reach the destination one set out to go to."

"True. We should be at Srirangam in a few hours. Since the Sri Ranganath Swamy temple is just a few kilometres from it, why don't we go there today itself and visit the temple fresh in the morning?"

"Sounds good. Coming back to Mahabharat, once Arjun was persuaded to pick up his weapon again, the war started in right earnest. But why did Pandavas have to resort to unfair means to eliminate the top Kaurava stalwarts?" DK came straight to the point.

"Once again we need to admire Krishna's strategic mastery," JT pointed out patiently. "Just as Krishna had come to the conclusion that Kansa and Jarasandha were too evil to continue and that for the well-being of the ordinary citizenry they needed to be eliminated, so it was for Duryodhan and his backers as well. Even if they included venerable names like Bhishma and Dronacharya. To achieve that end result, Arjun's skill was required and Krishna very shrewdly ensured that it was harnessed to achieve the larger goal."

"Even the way Bhishma was killed?" DK wanted to know.

"There was no deception really in it. It was obvious by the ninth day of the war that as long as Bhishma was fighting on behalf of Kauravas, Pandavas could not win. Using Shikhandi as a front the next day was a smart tactic, it can't really be Pandavas' or Krishna's fault if Bhishma refused to fight Shikhandi."

"But then what about the killing of Guru Dronacharya? Surely the method used was most foul?"

"Yudhishthir's lie? *Ashwatthama, naro wa kunjro wa?* After uttering the lie, Yudhishthir's chariot, which used to always hover a few inches above the earth came down to it with a thud? Surely Dronacharya could have seen that and made out the lie!"

"Ha ha, true that!"

"But let us leave levity aside and think of the larger message the incident conveys. See, there is always a conflict between Good and Evil. If Evil can use any method to achieve its aims, Legitimate or Illegitimate, Right or Wrong, True or False, Fair or Unfair and Good is tied down to using only legitimate means, it is like assigning a permanent handicap to Good. That does not sound fair and it isn't."

"Back to the old '*Does End justify the Means*' argument?"

"With a very important caveat though. We will come to that in a minute. See, as per the Mahabharat, Dwapar Yuga ended with the fall of Bhishma on the tenth day of the war. The shadow of Kali Yuga began creeping over the earth more or less with Dronacharya taking command of the Kaurava army after that. To prove his special merit to Duryodhan, Dronacharya used his divine weapons against the common soldiers, completely against the ethics of war prevalent then."

"Yes, much like the use of Napalm bomb or chemical weapons would be in our times."

"Not just that, he initiated *night time* fighting too, in complete violation of the then prevalent rules, which laid down that war was permitted only between sunrise and sunset."

"Sort of like what violating Geneva convention would mean today?"

"Exactly. It can never be that only one side follows a certain code and the other side is free to violate it. Natural justice would indicate that if one side does not play by the rules, it would relieve the other side of any obligation to do so also. Krishna had complete clarity on this and guided Pandavas appropriately, for under Yudhishthir, they sometimes tended to overemphasise the *means* at the cost of attaining the overall objective."

"Once the premise of *means* being given primacy over the *end* in specific situations is accepted, there is no reason really to discuss the ends of other important figures like Karna or Duryodhan."

"Sure but here too the strategic acumen of Krishna shines through. The moment *night war* was initiated by Dronacharya, Krishna used it masterfully to eliminate the only real threat to Arjun and the Pandavas — Karna with Indra's *Vajra*."

"The one Karna had been blessed with by Indra Dev for parting with the '*kavach kundala*'?"

"Yes. You will remember that Dronacharya started the night war with the intention of kidnapping Yudhishthir; Krishna turned the situation around to his advantage by unleashing Bheem's son Ghatotkach, from the *rakshasi* Hidimba. Ghatotkach's powers increased manifold during the night and the havoc he caused in the Kaurav army led to Duryodhan pleading with Karna to use his *Vajra* against Ghatotkach, which he did."

DK nodded in agreement. "And as per Indra's terms, the *Vajra* was for one time use only. Once it was gone, there was no threat to Arjun really. Sacrificing a knight to save the queen, if one might use a harsh chess analogy."

"Fairly accurate," said JT with a laugh.

"One final question about Mahabharat itself. About Parikshit, Abhimanyu's son, being brought to life again by Krishna after Ashwatthama's Brahmastra killed him in his mother Uttara's womb."

"Yes, that narrative gives a lot of comfort to the devotees. And why not? To them, it is a ringing confirmation of Krishna's divinity. But others might wonder about a couple of things."

"Such as?" DK wanted to know.

"Whichever version you read, before Parikshit is brought back to life, Krishna is supposed to have said something like 'If I have always followed the path of Dharma, then may this child live.' That makes some people wonder that if Krishna was indeed divine, where was the need for such a qualification? He could simply have brought Parikshit to life without any ado. Was it a post-facto introduction in the texts seeking to bolster the argument in favour of Krishna's divine origins? Thought provoking at the very least."

"Now that we are discussing the incident, I am reminded of my niece's daughter. She was not breathing when she was born and doctors had to resort to Neonatal Resuscitation to get her to start breathing. It was successful too," DK recalled.

"Practically, every good maternity home or neonatal facility in India or anywhere in the world deals with such situations regularly. Remember, there is a growing belief that the birth of Kauravs has a lot of features of modern In Vitro Fertilisation or IVF methodology. It is resorted to fairly commonly by couples today in need of help in having a child. It would be very illogical to deny the possibility that some form of Neonatal Resuscitation too was practised in ancient India."

"Either way, it was great that Parikshit survived and went on to rule after Yudhishthir. You had mentioned about one caveat while discussing 'Means versus Ends' a while back. What was it all about? I must confess that the inherent logic of this 'Means Versus Ends' argument bothers me; who, after all, is to be the judge of *when or under what circumstances* can cutting corners and using dicey methods be justified citing some noble objective?" DK looked troubled.

"Do you play Bridge?" JT asked.

"What? Yes I do sometimes play socially at the club. What does that have to do with our discussion?"

"You must have noticed that all good players follow certain well established rules while playing the game; from simple ones like second plays low, third plays high to more advanced ones like using probability of various distribution patterns to even more advanced ones like the theory of Restricted Choice."

"I don't know the last one, but I understand what you are saying. What I still don't get is what you are driving at."

"Simple. While all good players follow established principles, only the experts know when to play against the probabilities or when to break the rules or come up with outlandish plays."

"Aah, now I get a glimmer of what you are saying."

"See, if you were to watch an all expert bridge game, very easy to do today on the internet, you will be shocked. Bluff, double bluff, discards of aces, under-ruffing when opponents have already ruffed, all sorts of unusual plays can be seen. Sometimes such deals take long to analyse afterwards and ordinary mortals like us wonder how the expert thought of it on the spur of the moment at the table."

"I know the feeling absolutely," said DK with a grimace.

"Coming back to your question. The question of when to break the rules, when to cut corners to achieve legitimate goals is best left to the experts, or in the social context, to the leaders. It is one thing for the leader of a country to decide that certain corners can be cut while dealing with another country in pursuit of some national goals; it would be quite another for a student to claim the same privilege and cheat in his school exams simply because his objective, that of passing the exams, is a good one too, from his point of view."

"Hmm... I get the distinction. What you are saying in effect is that it would not be okay for a common man to invoke Krishna and Gita and start violating established norms."

"Absolutely. If everyone thinks Krishna or Gita gave her or him a general licence to cut corners, it would be a huge mistake and society would collapse in no time at all. For 99 per cent of the people, Ram is the better ideal to follow; how to be an ideal son or husband or brother or even a king. Krishna's message is really for the exceptional leader, just like him."

"Could that be the reason why keeping a copy of Mahabharat at home is discouraged in large parts of India, especially in the north?"

"Yes, many believe that reading it could bring discord in the family so it is best to avoid having a copy at home."

"Let us get back to Krishna for a bit. After the war some very poignant incidents have been narrated in most versions of Mahabharat about Gandhari holding Krishna responsible for the war and indirectly at least, for the death of her children."

"See, Pandavas may have won the war but it had left everyone unhappy. Even Pandavas, for they had lost many children, close relatives, friends and lakhs of soldiers. Kingdoms far and near had suffered loss of lives on a scale never seen before. And Krishna, who many had started revering as an *avataar*, an incarnation of God himself, was at the centre of it all. Therefore, many people blamed him for the carnage. Seen in that light, Gandhari's grief and outpouring was not unnatural."

"Not just Gandhari. Even sages like Uttanka are said to have been very upset with Krishna," DK probed further.

"Yes, there were many who were genuinely troubled as to how such a huge manslaughter could have taken place in his presence. You could even say that they were too close to the events to grasp the complex Good versus Evil drama which had just played out. And obviously there had been no time for the message of Gita to reach the leaders of the society, leave alone its percolating down to the common people or even sages dwelling in forests."

"In any case it would be unfair to expect a mother like Gandhari to have been convinced about the venality of her children," DK said thoughtfully.

"That reminds me. A little while back I had said there were only two people in Mahabharat who were never in a dilemma about their decision making. One was Krishna. He was such a genius that in any given situation he could arrive at the correct decision in a flash. Where others were troubled by contradictory calls of duty, Krishna was never in trouble because his concepts, his thinking were completely sorted, and he always knew which was the correct course of action, which among the many conflicting duties deserved priority in any given circumstances. And, most important, he never lost."

"Hmmm. And the second one?" asked DK although by now he could sense the answer.

"The second one was Duryodhan," said JT. "He was never in two minds about what he should do because only his duty towards himself, his self-interest, mattered to him. To achieve that, every other duty or relationship could be sacrificed without a thought."

"Gandhari was obviously voluntarily blind and not just physically. One can't argue with a mother's love. It is pure, unconditional and often unreasoning," DK rationalised.

"Which may be the reason why Krishna is shown accepting Gandhari's accusations, even her curse, with equanimity but without argument."

"She cursed Krishna that his Yadav clan will also self-destruct like the Kauravas had almost done and yes, Krishna is said to have taken it all stoically. One thing puzzles me though. Why did it take 36 years for the curse to become effective?"

JT shrugged. "It is hard to find any reason. There can't be a standard measure in such matters but it probably weakens the case for Krishna's divine origins. If eradication of Evil was the purpose of the *avataar*, that purpose had already been served with the death of Duryodhan and his cabal and installation of Yudhishthir as the king in the most dominant capital in Bharatvarsh, Hastinapur."

"I find the only notable events in that final 36 year period really very saddening. Sensing the imminent end of Dwarka, Krishna's sending an SOS to Arjun to take the ladies to safety someplace. And Arjun, the hero of Mahabharat, the one *Maharathi* who even Bhishma, Dronacharya or Karna could never defeat, being thrashed by ordinary goons on the way from Dwarka with the ladies." DK's anguish was plain.

"I guess it is intended to show that time spares no one."

DK was thoughtful. "Now that the subject of these ladies has come up, it reminds me. So much has been written about them, more than 16,000 of them, as Krishna's wives!"

JT sighed. "The legend of Narkasur."

“What exactly happened?”

“The legend can be summarised easily, at least the more common one. Narkasur was an evil king who is believed to have established the kingdom of Pragjyotish after killing off the last ruler of the Danava dynasty. He became all powerful and soon captured both heaven and earth. The power went to his head, he stole the earrings of Aditi, the heavenly mother goddess and also kidnapped 16,000 women.”

“Now I get where that 16,000 figure comes from.”

“Aditi appealed to Satyabhama, Krishna’s wife, who was related to her, and after a fierce battle between Satyabhama and Krishna on one side and Narkasur on the other, the latter was killed. The 16,000 women in his captivity were freed.”

“And the veracity of the story?”

“See, versions of Narakasur story can be found in literature from mid first millennium BCE, although the most elaborate treatment is probably given in Kalika Purana of the 10th century. About veracity, since the supposed events relate to Dwapar Yuga and were first written about thousands of years later, it may be best that we move on to our real focus, Krishna.”

“Yes, but did Krishna really marry 16,00 women?” DK persisted

“Even the way the story comes to us, it does nothing but glorify Krishna. At the end of all the fighting and after Narkasur’s death, the 16,000 women found themselves in a pitiful condition, at the mercy of a none-too-sympathetic society. It is Krishna who gives them respectability with his name and sustenance for life.”

“Now I understand. Those who view the story with salacious interest surely deserve to be ignored. Let us get back to where we left Arjun getting thrashed while escorting these women to safety 36 years after the war.”

"As I said, it is intended to show that time spares no one."

"Indeed not even Krishna himself. The story of his being mistaken for a stag and being shot through his sole by a hunter in Bhalka is too well known to need repetition."

"What an end to the most heroic person to have walked on land ever." The tinge of sadness in JT's voice was unmistakable.

Dusk was setting in and lights of Srirangam could be seen as they passed through the town. The temple was just a few kilometres beyond, the end of the long journey seemed to be in sight. There was silence for a few minutes before DK could bring himself up to take up the conversation again.

"Tell me, for the last few days we have tried to see if it was possible to explain away all that has come down to us about Krishna without necessarily having to fall back upon *divine origins* as an answer; and it looks like, yes, there are alternate explanations. So does that make Krishna a larger or a smaller figure than the *divine origins* explanation would have?"

"In my view, definitely a larger, more inspiring figure. See, human beings need larger-than-life role models to understand what is possible. Once you bring in divinity, you are talking of the impossible. Krishna becomes someone from another world. People will fold their hands, remember him on special days like Janmashtami every year and forget about him for the rest."

"And if the belief in Krishna's divine origins is kept aside?"

"Then he becomes someone who people can attempt to emulate no matter how high benchmarks he has set. It may be a poor example but see, if there had been no Donald Bradman, people would never have believed that an average close to 100 in Test cricket is possible even after a long career. In many walks of life there have been people who have achieved extraordinary feats that serve to inspire generations to try and match them."

"And Krishna?"

"While most great people have set extraordinary standards in one field, here is someone who has set an almost impossible benchmark in every aspect of life. Complete 360 degrees. He achieved perfection as a friend, philosopher and guide to Pandavas. But well before that too, his life demonstrates perfection in conceiving and executing strategies no matter what the odds. Not just while dealing with Kansa or Jarasandha, even while dealing with situations concerning the shift to Dwarka or his marriage to Rukmini; throughout his whole life really, Krishna has demonstrated Perfection. That is why he is often referred to as *Purnavataar*, a descriptive term which can be used even if the thought of his divine origin is kept aside as someone who has demonstrated Complete Perfection in all aspects of Life."

"So what is a common person to make of Krishna and the high benchmark he has set?" DK spoke as if in a trance.

"The biggest tribute to Krishna would be for people to strive to achieve perfection in whatever they do. A singer who attempts and perfects a particular note, in effect, becomes Krishna for that moment. An architect who conceives and executes a building plan to perfection becomes Krishna for the moment; a carpenter who completes a piece of furniture to perfection becomes Krishna for the moment; a cook who cooks the perfect dish becomes Krishna... for the moment. It is enough for an ordinary individual to try and maximise the 'Krishna moments' in his life. Achieving perfection even for a few moments would be a marvellous tribute to the greatest man to ever walk on earth. It may not be possible for ordinary mortals to think of managing perfection 24x7x 365 but even achieving it in small bits and pieces would be great and a reward in itself. The ultimate would be to use every microsecond of time available to try and become Krishna in whatever one does. Even if that goal appears impossible."

DK let that sink in for a while. Minutes went by before he could bring himself to speak again. It was as if he had just understood the very secret and purpose of life itself.

"It has been such a wonderful, wonderful journey JT, I can't begin to thank you," said DK as *nandighosh* pulled into the petrol pump in the shadow of the majestic Sri Ranganath Swamy Temple. Even in the fading light the imposing structure was most impressive.

"I have enjoyed it thoroughly too," replied JT.

"Let us have a good night's rest before taking *darshan* of the deity tomorrow morning," said DK.

❑❑❑

Epilogue

DK woke up with a start and looked at the bright sunlight streaming through the window curtains. How could I be late, he thought and then remembered. Neeta had called around midnight and said that they needed to take Meera to the hospital. Looking at the position of the baby's head and the lessening quantity of fluid, her doctor had advised them not to take any chances. He had tossed and turned a bit in worry and then must have dozed off. They must have reached the hospital by now, a new day in my life, literally and figuratively and I am starting late, he thought as he stepped into the bathroom.

JT was nowhere to be seen, must have gone ahead, DK thought as he put on a mask and started for the Sri Ranaganath Swamy temple complex 20 minutes later. Spread over 156 acres with a perimeter in excess of four kilometres, it was truly breath-taking. Thankfully, the crowd was sparse. Covid-19 fear was still around and the management seemed to be taking all precautions. In a few minutes, he had entered the impressive sanctum sanctorum. He did his namaskar to the idol of Ranganath, a reclining form of Bhagwan Vishnu, dropped a bundle of Rs 10,000/- in the massive steel donation box and moved forward to receive the *prasad* from the head priest. He cupped his hand and looked up into the smiling, twinkling, old eyes.

"I have come a long way in search of some answers Guruji," DK said with bowed head.

The elderly priest ladled out the *prasad* liquid into DK's hand, kept the ladle aside and placed his hand on DK's head.

"You do not need any more answers son, the ability to ask searching questions itself is a sign of adequate awakening. People forget so easily that Arjun also played a key role in Bhagwad Gita by asking the right questions. You have already gained some knowledge, it is time for *prasad grahan*."

DK sipped the liquid thinking about the priest's words and stepped out of the sanctum sanctorum. He looked around to see if he could locate JT and his phone rang.

"Congratulations grandfather of a bonny grandson," Neeta could not contain her excitement.

"What!" DK could hardly speak, he was overcome with emotion.

"7 pounds, 19 inches tall, very good looking with features just like mine, so says everyone," said Neeta primly.

"Lucky him," said DK. A strange calm enveloped him. "What have they named him?"

Meera and Naresh had wanted to keep it a secret till the birth, although they had provided options to the hospital as legally mandated locally.

"Mohan," said Neeta. "Meera and Naresh did not want a new-fangled Aryan or something. Besides it had to be easy for Americans to pronounce."

"Can't go wrong with Mohan," said DK. He smiled to himself. Was it fated, he wondered. The perfect finale to his journey, physical and mental, which had started with another Mohan. Mohan Bhargava, Shah Rukh Khan's screen persona in the film *Swades*. "Let me see when I can come over. I think some airline routes via Europe are opening up. Let me check, I don't want to wait anymore! I will call you later in the day."

DK stepped out of the temple complex and still could not see any sign of JT. Very unlike him, DK thought, as his mind went over their conversation last night just before they had turned in.

"It has been a wonderful trip so far JT. Maybe we could do some more such trips together. How do I contact you? I don't even have your mobile number."

"I don't carry one. But *jab bhi aap yaad karoge, hum aa jaayenge*!" JT had said with a smile.

DK was puzzled. He looked at his wrist watch, took out his phone, opened Google to check flight timings to Mumbai. He checked the driving time to Tiruchirapalli. He checked his watch for the tenth time since leaving the temple as he entered *nandighosh*. The second 'bedroom' was empty.

JT must have meant he could be contacted through Ahuja thought DK. Maybe Ahuja knows where he has gone and tapped his speed dial.

"How are you Ahuja, *kaise hain*?"

"*Bas aapki dua hai DK sahab*." The voice sounded very weak.

"*Maain Thakurji ko dhoondh raha hoon, unhone aapko contact kiya kya*?"

"*Kaun Thakurji*?"

"Same Jagganath Thakurji that you had sent to me eight days ago as a companion-cum-driver. We reached our destination in Srirangam yesterday, I need to make his payment and plan the journey back," DK was now getting impatient.

"Sorry DK *sahab*, there seems to be some mistake. The Janardan Thakur that I had recommended had tested positive for Covid one day before you were to leave and I was also down with severe Covid for last eight days. I was feeling bad for having let you down, but I was in an ICU with many tubes stuck into me and no mobile phones were allowed. They shifted me into the private room from the ICU just this morning."

"But then who was the Jagganath Thakur who accompanied me for the last eight days? Wonderful man, very knowledgeable!" DK exclaimed.

"My office must have sent him after Janardan Thakur's Covid report came positive. *Jaane dijiye ji, Janardan, Jagganath ki pharak painda hai, donon ikkoi gal hai! Apka kaam ho gaya na,* that is all that matters. And don't worry about his payment, *jab contact karega*, my office will take care of it and send you the bill. *Aur koi hukum*?"

DK set aside Thakur, Jagganath or Janardan, for the present as his mind jumped to the happier task.

"You had said you can arrange a driver anywhere in India?"

"Anytime, anywhere."

Dhananjay Kuru cleared his mind, he was feeling completely relaxed, completely satisfied that he understood everything.

"Can you arrange to send someone to Tiruchirapalli airport in two hours please? He can take my two door vanity van back to Mumbai. I need to catch a flight to Mumbai and from there to USA.I have a bonny grandson there now, a new Mohan in my life and I am seeing the world in an entirely different light."

❑❑❑

About the Authors

Satish Mutatkar

An alumnus of prestigious academic institutions BITS, Pilani and Faculty of Management Studies, Delhi University, Satish Mutatkar moved from a sterling corporate career after 15 years and turned to the creative world. Over the last thirty years and more, he has Written, Directed and Produced TV Serials, TVCs and Corporate films. He has also written songs for Hindi films, most notably V.G. Samant's 'Hanuman', Anurag Kashyap's 'Return of Hanuman', both animation films targeted at children and Priyadarshan's Hindi adaptation of the Oscar nominated Iranian film 'Children of Heaven' by Majid Majidi.

Among the chartbusters, Mutatkar has written include 'Asmaan ko Chukar Dekha' sung by Daler Mehendi, 'Mahabali Maharudra' sung by a galaxy of singers including Sonu Nigam, Shaan, Kailash Kher, Vijay Prakash, Palash Sen, Tapas Relia, Madhushree, Sneha Pant, Sapna Mukherjee and 'Akdam Bakdam' sung by Shravan.

Mutatkar has been Principal Consultant to ISRO for a proposed Science Channel Project and has also been a columnist for DNA online.

❑❑❑

Authorspeak

I owe a serious debt of gratitude to many people for making this book happen.

First, to my co-author Yeshwant Marathe. When he approached me with the idea, I was intrigued and I can say with all honesty that if I had known how much time would be needed for the research and writing, I might have said thank you, but no thank you. And then he persisted gently, without losing his smile or equanimity once, till the journey was complete.

Next, I need to thank Praveen Rattan, my friend from Pilani days in the late 1960s and early 70s when we did Electronics Engineering together. Professional writing has sometimes been defined as rewriting and rewriting. It is not possible without a very diligent and competent sounding board, which Praveen has been for me, so selflessly and for so long. There are other friends also from so many Pilani WA groups who shared lots of *gyaan* about our epics over the years, here's a collective thank you to all of them too.

Finally, to all my family members, Madhavi, Sheela, Meghana, Rohit, Shivani and Advait, thank you for being so supportive throughout. And how can I forget my two heartthrobs, granddaughter Aria and grandson Riaan, without whose intrusions into my study the book might have been finished three months earlier but might have missed out on some extra insights which only association with grandchildren can provide?

I dedicate this book to my late elder sister, Shashikala Mutatkar, remembered every day.

Satish Mutatkar

Yeshwant Marathe

Yeshwant Marathe is a third generation businessman from the house of Marathe Udyog. He is the Managing Trustee of Neeraja Foundation, working for Community Level Rainwater Harvesting by constructing bunds, repairing defunct check dams, repairing wells and cleaning ponds in rural India.

Marathe is also a prolific Blogger. His Marathi Blog *Sarmisal* (सरमिसळ), covers a wide range of subjects under the categories of Culture, Affairs, Philosophy, Nostalgia, Word Sketches and Travelogue. His English Blog History Cafe explores nuggets from history. A book of his selected Marathi articles was published under the title 'छपाई ते लेखणी' in December 2020. Readers seem to love his easy, informal language and analytical yet humorous approach.

❑❑❑

Authorspeak

I am overwhelmed that our efforts of last two years are finally seeing the light of the day. I have had so many sleepless nights during this period, some due to despair and others due to excitement and it is time to thank all those who held my hand during the journey.

At the outset, I must thank Paresh Sukhtankar who connected me to Satish Mutatkar. This book would not have happened without that intervention. Then I must thank Bhagwan Joshi and Chinmay Thakar who gave me frank, unbiased feedback on the many ideas I bounced off them. There are so many other friends who kept on encouraging all the while, it is impossible to name everyone but here's a big 'thanks' to them all.

My family has been a constant source of encouragement but special thanks to Aditi for being a pillar of strength and for being my most vocal critic. The other members too need to be thanked for helping me stay the course. And yes, I have to make a special mention of my grandson Arin, whose entry in my life delayed the book by few months but I have no complaints at all.

Finally, to my co-author, Mr Satish Mutatkar. What can I say of such a talented wizard who is a Sportsman by heart, Engineer by profession and later a renowned English and Hindi Writer, Lyricist, TV Commercials, TV Serials and Corporate film maker? The art of storytelling which is so evident in this book is all thanks to him.

I dedicate this book to my late father, Suresh Marathe, who inspired so many, including me.

Yeshwant Marathe